Your Marron is out there. You deserve to be

loved and cherished.

Copyright

This book is a work of fiction. It is a modern reimagination of many mythologies. None of it is designed to be factual. All content and information in this book belongs to Jessica Lane, published 08/23/2023. Any replication is unauthorized.

CHAPTER 1

The Creature trudged through the puddles consuming the sidewalk. "Creature" that's what the people had begun calling it. The being had adopted that moniker as its own now as well. No longer had it been able to shift into anything that resembled something familiar. Its true form lost from memory. If it thought long and hard about the subject, perhaps its last attempt was a cat, but now its ears flopped like a dog and its tail wound in a loose coil, dragging in the filthy water behind it. A calico disgrace. It wasn't entirely sure what its eyes resembled. Glimpses of its reflection led the creature to believe one of its pupils was slit, like a snake. The other was pure brown and devoid of a pupil altogether.

A young fae girl, ice cream dripping down her chin, pointed at the creature with concern. "Momma… Its aura, Momma…It's black…"

The Creature groaned. It could feel its claws scraping the pavement as it walked. *Great, just what it needed.* Fae children were blessed with the gift of being able to see others' auras, though most grew out of it by the time they reached puberty. It wasn't often that children ran across a black aura, so Creature had become accustomed to pointed fingers and statements of shock. *Death follows me.*

The mother patted her daughter's pink frizz, "Well, if it were me, I'd welcome the omen…" she sneered while ushering her small child away.

Creature *did* welcome death. If only Hades, God of the Underworld, would heed its appeals. The crows all watched the creature but made no movement towards it.

The creature spotted a coffee shop, moving to lay under the balcony window in what appeared to be the only dry spot in the entire city.

Scynthia was a loud bustle of fae and humans as the Norse, Greek, Roman, Celtic, and Indigenous gods of the Americas had struck a treaty creating the Scynthian realm. There was everything one could want or need, but mostly Scynthia acted as neutral grounds for gods, fae, and humans to conduct business together. The embassy sat in the center of the city. Because humans could not fade, or teleport, from one place to another, buses and cars filled the streets.

The creature closed its eyes and listened to the city's chaos, lulled to sleep by the surrounding urban cacophony. A disturbingly chipper voice roused it but a few moments later.

"Good afternoon, Bill!" A woman carrying a grand bouquet of flowers called out to a passerby. "Oh, dear gods, who are *you*?" The feminine voice was much too close this time. Creature jumped and hit its head on the window box, releasing a close approximation of a cat's hiss.

The approaching woman's tight, lilac curls perfectly framed her deeply tanned and freckled cheeks. Her vibrant green stare radiated pure kindness and patience as she reached out a hand to the creature. "My dear, I'd like to buy you something to eat if you will allow it."

Creature plopped its behind firmly on the ground and canted its head towards the woman.

"You are absolutely right. I failed to introduce myself." The woman pressed her hand to her chest in apology for the offense. "That is quite rude of me. My name is Meraena. I am a mer fae. Pleased to meet you."

The Creature just stared at the woman. Her dark skin shimmered in the summer sun, just now peeking from behind the rain clouds. She wore a pearlescent white dress that must have been tailored to her exact measurements, hugging her curves. It was covered in a delicate floral lace pattern. Why would a woman such as her deign to speak to something such as Creature?

"We have shifters in the seas…" She looked down, empathy filling her eyes. "They get stuck too, as I gather you to be stuck in this form. Time and patience…and the right company helps, of course."

The Creature stood and approached the beautiful woman.

Meraena smiled and winked. "Wonderful! I just got off work, so let's get a bite to eat. Then we can go to my apartment. Perhaps some rest and a safe place will help you shift again." She stood effortlessly and smoothed her dress fastidiously, in a manner suggestive of a wealthy upbringing.

Meraena tilted her head towards the café and

held the door open for the beast. The Creature hesitated and looked up at her figure as she waited patiently with the door resting against her hips. It padded slowly through, relishing the coolness of the tile floors below its feet. Old brick walls wrapped around the interior, Edison lights strung across the ceiling added to the warm urban atmosphere, as the lush smell of coffee filled the air. Elegant sofas, armchairs and tables were filled with patrons.

Creature immediately felt out of place, which was only reinforced when almost immediately an angry shout came from behind the glass and metal counter.

"No animals in my cafe, lady! I do nae care if they were once shifters, that thing is a filthy disgrace to the fae community and is nae welcome here." The burly man, with an apron covered in espresso splatter and icing, chastised- his Scottish accent thick as he pointed a large finger at Creature. This was not an uncommon occurrence. Fae disowned their kin who could not master their gifts in adolescence. It had seen numerous mixed formed shifters on the street through the years. To be fair, Creature had blocked out the truth of why it was stuck like this. Was it but a pup? It could be, perhaps, but in its core, it felt older… worn… used.

"Well, Shamus, that is a crying shame. I would hate to hear that my father's business with you and yours finally ceased after seventy-five years of friendship. We sure do love what you do with our crab and seaweed each summer solstice. Oh my, isn't that coming up next week?" Meraena began reaching into her purse.

Creature watched as Shamus' face filtered through seven different shades of red. "Fine," he grumbled finally. "But it sits on a towel, and you toss the towel in the rubbish when you are done."

"Ah, you're in luck, Shamus. I want my food to go. You would have known had you not started barking at me first. Now, I want an iced dirty chai latte, an everything bagel, and whatever my friend indicates it wants through the glass."

Creature paused and looked up at the woman. For the past few years, it had subsisted on trash finds from the alley and whatever it could catch in the fields. What would it know of this food? Creature walked to the bakery display and sat a bit disheveled, peering at the host of options. The bread with meat on it should suffice. Creature got as close to that selection without touching the glass and grunted at Meraena. The Mer smiled and informed Shamus she wanted *three* of those sandwiches. Creature balked.

It waited silently by the door as Meraena paid. Different fae filtered in and out of the place, though very few sat down to eat. Most of the patrons had a laptop, cell phone, or a book pulled out. This was a common sight in Scynthia now that fae and humans had reached an agreement on their peace treaty. Human technology had filtered up to the fae and was used interchangeably when needed. It was common for fae and the gods to wish to retain the ethereal aesthetic in their realms, the adoption of technology into Scythia and other realms was a slow progression. Creature wasn't even sure it remembered how to read anymore, let alone manage a piece of technology.

"Meraena," Shamus called and placed a bag and drink on the counter. He met her eyes, almost apologetically, but frowned at the food instead, dropping his gaze from hers.

She nodded and turned towards the door. "Come on, friend. Let's go home."

Home: what a thought. Meraena turned out to live only two blocks away, in a brick-laid gated apartment complex. Creature paused at the gate, an opulent golden work of art. Welded vines and leaves wove through the bars. Few cars trekked down the road. Grand trees lined the sidewalks, with songbirds tweeting happily. It was clear this was a complex that belonged to those of Greek and Roman descent.

Places like this were often warded against lesser fae. Creature snaked a paw through the gate hesitantly, pleased to discover the move wasn't followed by a painful zap.

"Hmm. Interesting." Meraena peered down at her new companion. "Alright. Here's the plan of attack for the night. We are going to eat first. Then, I'll help you get clean. I'm not sure the last time you had a proper bath, but that is a must before we proceed in my home. Next, it's a movie and bed. I am off work tomorrow, so perhaps we can filter through some animals you'd be interested in shifting to. Maybe find a singular form for you to take on."

The Creature nodded. What else could it do?

They walked down the bright green carpeted hallway until they came upon a hot pink door labeled as 2A. It was surrounded with foliage and pots brimming with various flowers.

"I'm a botanist." Meraena smiled with pride and ran her fingers along the fuchsia bleeding hearts next to her doorbell. She unlocked the door and began turning lights on in her apartment.

Creature was met with a beautiful home. It made note of the hardwood floors with white accent rugs. It was sure to give them a wide berth. Gold light fixtures brightened the ceilings. A light scent of lilac and cinnamon filled the air. The couch was a soft lavender color with a crystal coffee table placed in front. The creature followed Meraena into the kitchen. A small island ran down the center of the open kitchen/dining room layout. It was there that Creature's host set down her meal, grabbing plates from the cabinets behind her.

A bit at a loss, Creature sat on the wooden floor.

"Let's go to the table." She placed a towel atop the gold-trimmed glass table and placed the plate with Creature's sandwich next to it.

Creature jumped onto the towel and took a hesitant bite of the food. Meraena watched the being as she ate her bagel. Creature's body began humming unwittingly as it ate. It looked at Meraena in confusion, deli meat still hanging from its mouth.

She laughed. "You are purring. You must be enjoying your food."

Creature nodded and continued to eat and purr, whatever that meant.

They finished their meals and Meraena cleaned up the dishes. Once done, she filled one side of the sink with soapy water and announced, "Bath time."

Creature walked over and allowed the Mer to lift its body to the sink.

"Put your paw in and see if the temperature is ok. I don't want it to be too hot or cold for you."

Creature obeyed and placed its paw in the water before stepping all the way in and closing its eyes. It couldn't remember the last time it had felt such luxury.

It sat in the warm water and began involuntarily purring again. Meraena gave it a moment of peace before she said, "I am going to begin washing you now."

Creature looked up at the female and nodded. It didn't mean to, perhaps it was rude in some way, but the creature fell asleep in the water with its head on the Mer's forearm as she scrubbed and washed it clean. Creature had forgotten what it was to feel such comfort and slept clear through the remainder of the evening.

CHAPTER 2

"Good morning." Meraena smiled at Creature. "I really want a name for you. Can we begin with that this morning?"

Creature nodded. It thought a name aside from Creature would be lovely.

"Perfect. Are you a male or female?"

Creature looked away from Meraena. It no longer remembered.

"That's okay. There are dual names out there. Let's think…hmm. Rae?" Creature shook its head. "Wren?" Creature shrugged. "Eden?" Creature perked up.

Meraena grinned. "Eden it is. I'm starving, Eden. Let's find something to eat, huh?"

Suddenly, the front door flew open, and a giant mass of a man barreled into the room. "Meraena, I swear if I have to listen to *one* more gods-damned thing I've failed to – what in the underworld is *that*?"

Meraena grunted, apparently unbothered at the man seeing her in pajamas and sleep-disheveled hair.

"Marron, this is Eden. We met yesterday. He or she may very well think what in the underworld are *you*, so be respectful! We are going to work on shifting into one form today, hopefully." She offered a kind smile to Eden. "Eden, this is Marron, crown annoying prince of Phrygia. What he's doing in my apartment on a Saturday morning before my morning coffee, is beyond me."

Marron's broad, muscular body was fitted in a blue satin dress shirt and black slacks that screamed of wealth. He eyed Eden's dog-like ears cautiously before proceeding. "Oh, nothing, just the king and politics and war and my incessant bride to be. If I have to hear about the color chartreuse one more time, my brain might actually melt. No one in Asgard will acknowledge the threat of war. Loki is going to destroy their entire realm; it's not a matter of *if* it happens, just *when*. He's festering about something. I can feel it. Something that he's looking for." Marron began flipping the dagger hanging from his belt while pacing the living room and staring at the ceiling above.

Meraena started the coffee pot and put

something in the oven, Eden was not sure what. "My father will not get involved in the wars of Phrygia and Asgard. Your father is wise to let Loki create his own chaos. That is not a concern of ours at this moment."

"It will be if Loki has no realm to threaten…" Marron flopped down on the couch in the most unprincely manner Eden had ever seen. "I need a beer."

"Again, it's 7 a.m." Meraena gave him a side eye and poured out two cups of coffee, handing one to the man on her couch. "Coffee is the place to start. How is Kornelia?"

Marron grunted into his mug. "Not a woman fit to be at my side. She cries at the sight of mothers and babies. The discussion of war makes her run to the bathroom with a sick stomach. How is such a soft woman supposed to rule a kingdom? I've been doing my best obnoxious act, hoping she will beg her father to end the agreement, but it has yet to be effective." He ran a rough hand through his autumn red hair.

Eden felt uneasy but attributed it to hunger as it sensed its stomach growl immediately after. Meraena pulled a tray out of the oven and placed a plate of something she declared to be bacon on the table. Marron all but ran to the table, so it followed suit. The prince's shoulder-length wavy ginger hair hung loose, framed by a few braids with gold beads woven into their ends. He swung it back from his face as he tipped a cup of coffee into his mouth. The bacon smelled delicious. Meraena handed Eden a plate and sat herself across the table from Marron. She cradled her mug with both hands and stared at the steam rising from it.

"Eden, huh?" Eden looked up at the Prince. "Are you a woman shifter defect?"

"Marron, if you cannot be kind, then *leave*." Meraena's eyes had turned into steel.

"I was just asking… Eden is a feminine name." Marron's deep ocean-blue eyes watched as Eden ate the bacon. It bared its teeth around the bite. He bared his. Canines dropping lower from his gums. "Careful who you threaten, *thing.*"

"That's it, Marron. Get out of my apartment until you can learn some manners."

Marron sighed and grabbed a piece of bacon before heading towards the door. "Meraena, I'm… It's just a bad day. Eden, I'm sorry. Next time will be better."

"There will not *be* a next time if it is not better, Marron. I don't care if you are my best friend and ally." Meraena held his stare until the prince bowed his head.

"Yes, your highness."

Eden canted its head at Meraena.

"My father is Poseidon. Prince Marron and I have known one another for one hundred years. We have survived many things through our friendship."

Eden nodded. It could understand that. Kinship was vital to the survival of royals, it supposed. The thought of intruding on a prince and princess' lives shook Eden to its core.

It couldn't become one to rely on the condition of its lodging. What a nuisance they would think of the being. If not now, then in time. What if it never shifted back? It would not be a being that uses those around it for its sole benefit.

What could Creature give back anyway? It did not deserve to live in such a place, with such a fae. Eden was a defect who had lived on the streets and in ramshackle homes for countless years. It was no one. A princess deigning to care and aid the beast-it was unseemly in truth. Eden jumped down from the table and went to stand by the door, staring at Meraena.

"What? Do you want to go outside? You may use my restroom, or I suppose I could get a litter box if you wish." Meraena stared at Eden who was pawing the door. "Okay, let's go."

Meraena nodded and donned pajama pants before opening the door. The two trekked down the effervescent hallway and out the front doors. Eden needed to leave, and quickly. Meraena was kind, but that didn't mean that it should waste her time on a probable lost cause.

In that moment Eden ran. It did not know where it ran to, but it ran down the sidewalk as fast as it could. It did not look back and went until its lungs gave way. Unfortunately, that was only three blocks. Meraena slowly followed behind and sat on the sidewalk as Eden caught its breath.

"I am allowed to care for you even if I am a princess." Meraena watched the cars pass. "My brother… he was a shifter. When you live in the water, if you don't shift into aquatic life, you have a very short amount of time to get to the surface. His second shift was in his sleep, and he had just learned about birds in his elementary class. No one knew to be concerned. I found a hawk in his bed one morning… My father mourned for years. I don't know how to fix you, but damn it I am going to try. However, you have to be willing to accept the help."

Eden felt tears run down its cheeks and leaned into Meraena.

"You are someone. Probably not Eden. Probably someone who can give Marron hell, which I will pay good money to see, but the fact that the wards on my apartment let you in tells me you once meant a great deal to someone in power. I don't think we want to focus on that today, though. Do you wish to be a cat? Is it a small animal you wish to be?"

Eden thought. It pawed its ears.

"A dog. Ok. We can start there. Let's go home and look into what kind of dog fits your fancy." Meraena reached down and scooped up Eden as if it was nothing and took it inside her apartment.

She immediately went to her room, which could only be described as pristine luxury; soft pinks and coral walls made the room feel bright and happy and the ever-white bed just emphasized the clean and elegant style Meraena embodied. It was as if she brought the coral reef to her bedroom. Scythian buildings and apartments lacked the grandeur of the godly realms. Creature supposed it was to make the humans feel more welcome.

Meraena opened her laptop and began searching for different breeds of dogs. Immediately, they were able to rule out small breeds such as chihuahuas and dachshunds.

"Eden, my friend, I do believe you are done being small." Eden rubbed against its friend's arm in confirmation. A picture of a malamute crossed Meraena's screen and Eden placed a paw on it. "Hmm. A shift like that will take time. All right, I am going to work on some research on the breed. Then, we will get started."

Eden wasn't sure why Meraena said the

statement as if it was going to leave the Mer's side. Where could it go? Three blocks before running out of air was rather pitiful.

It studied every canine picture the woman pulled up, every detail of the breed's musculature, skeletal structure, lineage, and coloring. It closed its eyes and focused on its tail. Maybe that would be a good place to start.

Pain surged through Eden, causing it to yelp and throw itself off the bed. Looking down, Eden saw the very tip of its tail was now gray and white, but alas – it was still a coiled disaster. Eden flopped onto the floor, defeated.

Meraena fought back a smile, maybe even a laugh. "I don't think shifting works one bit at a time. I think we might need to consult an actual shifter for this."

Eden grumbled and buried its head in the hardwood floor that smelled entirely too pleasant for how it felt.

Eventually, Meraena and Eden left the apartment and found their way to Meraena's city office.

It was a giant building made mostly of windows, each one surrounded by ivy and plant growth.

"We are trying to find ways to provide sustainable plant life in metropolitan areas. I personally study the coral reef and bringing it back to its full potential." She tucked her thick curls behind her ears and smiled as they crossed the bright white threshold.

Overall, Meraena's building was some hybrid between a hospital and a skyscraper with copious amounts of plants hanging from every possible location.

"Sometimes, I like to pretend I am in a rain forest." Meraena motioned to her left and walked towards the enchanting scent of lavender and lemon.

After grabbing pastries and coffee from the small built-in café, they found Meraena's office. As if to prove her earlier statement, tanks with varying light types lined the walls. Each tank had a wide range of coral and sea life thriving and interacting with one another. Vibrant fish wove in and out of bright purple anemone. It seemed peaceful.

"Make yourself at home. I just have a few projects to complete before I return to the ocean for a few days." Meraena gestured to the open space in the office, and placed Eden's pastry on a side table next to a small plush teal chair.

Eden at the lemon scone as it watched Meraena type away. The clicking of the keypad must have lulled Eden to sleep because the next thing it knew, the creature was being gently shaken.

"Let's head home, yeah? I'm tired of staring at my computer screen." Meraena smiled down at Eden, her curls had fallen as the day had progressed.

Eden stretched and hopped off the chair. Glancing out the window, it was surprised to discover the sun had begun to set.

The walk home was quiet, but companionable. Meraena didn't force any conversation. She seemed to be thinking fervently to herself.

Once back in the apartment, Meraena returned to researching malamutes despite having said she was tired of computers. Eden let itself be consumed by its failure to shift. It wasn't even aware that Marron arrived at night with several pizzas stacked on his shoulders.

"Evan!" Meraena ran past Marron across the

room and wrapped herself around a man nearly twice her size standing behind the prince. His muscular arms wrapped around the Mer and lifted her from the floor as her legs hugged his waist. Meraena's hands wove into his dark brown hair. The male's violet eyes beheld the woman in his arms with a heat Eden had never seen before. The being averted its eyes as the couple embraced and their mouths found each other.

Marron looked at Eden and laughed. "I take it you have little experience with fated mates. Why the gods or fates or whatever mated a berserker and a mermaid, I will never understand, but here we are. Get a fucking room or I will eat all this pizza and drink all the beer!"

Evan broke the kiss, hands still firmly on his mate's ass as Meraena's hands stayed in his dark brown hair with her lips pressed to his neck. "Just because I get laid, does not give you permission to be an ass and drink everyone's booze."

Marron grunted and sat next to Eden on the couch. It huffed at the prince and moved to the other side, grumbling incoherently. Eden allowed itself to properly assess Marron now. His flowing braided auburn hair reminded her of Thor and Loki's descendants. Odd for one of Phrygia, a predominantly Turkish culture, especially the son of King Midas. However, the empire was under the authority of Mt. Olympus and many of its constituents observed Greek religious practices.

Marron was likely six and a half feet tall and shrouded in muscles. He was right that morning to warn Eden not to threaten him. The being couldn't win a battle against him on its best day, but what did it have to lose anyway? Marron looked at Eden and frowned. "I owe you an apology."

Eden simply nodded and huffed at its tail and its incomplete transformation.

"Ah, yes. That is one of the reasons we came tonight. I am a shifter. The first thing you learn as a young shifter is when you shift, it's your whole body- not one part at a time. If you do one part at a time, you run the risk of getting stuck like you are."

Eden grumbled again, and Marron chuckled.

"Let's try getting a drink in you and loosen you up. See if that helps. You were once a fae. It may help ease the stress."

Beer. Eden had never had alcohol to its knowledge. It stood, arched its back, jumped to the coffee table, and sat next to a beer can. Eden waited and stared at Marron. At this point it would give anything a shot.

Marron tipped his head back and let out a laugh. Eden thought he sounded like he needed one for a long time. "Come on, Eden."

He went into the kitchen and grabbed a bowl from the cabinet to the left of the sink. Eden looked around for Meraena and Evan, but the two had vanished.

"Give them an hour or so. They haven't seen each other in a month." Marron poured the amber liquid into the gold-flaked bowl and set it on the table. Eden watched the foam rise and then fall. It touched the foam with its paw and looked up at Marron quizzically as it licked the foam. Bitter…and sweet. Odd. The smell did nothing to encourage Eden to take a sip.

Eden lowered its mouth to the bowl, attempted to lap the beer up, and promptly choked on the foam invading its nose.

Marron laughed and dropped over the island, head falling on his arms as he roared in mirth. His laughter was loud enough to carry all the way to the upstairs neighbors, who stomped on their floor in protest. Eden jumped on the island furiously and rubbed its damp face on the prince's shoulder, leaving a smear of beer foam in its wake.

"Touché, Eden." He laughed. "Touché. Now wait for the foam to die down."

The creature whacked the prince with its tail as it hopped off the counter and back to the table. It watched the bubbles fall away and only then licked again at the liquid. The flavor was citric, like grapefruit. Eden took a few more licks.

"Slow down, Eden, we don't know your tolerance yet. Your body is small."

Eden growled at him and took one last sip before sitting on the table and fixing Marron with what it hoped he interpreted as a glare.

Marron shook his head with a smirk. "Gods, if only my betrothed had half of your spirit, Eden. I don't even know if you are a female or male, but she has the personality of a dry piece of pasta. I could tell her to jump out the window, and she just might. Take another drink. Then, I want you to picture the malamute in your mind. Don't break it down. Just picture it as one whole being."

Eden took another drink and shivered as the fizz went down. It focused on the picture of the malamute breed it had seen this morning, trying to bring forth the shift. It was almost there, it thought. Eden could almost feel the shift begin… Just then, Meraena and Evan reemerged from the bedroom. Their mixed scent interrupted everything and broke Eden's concentration. Eden huffed.

"Agreed." Marron scrunched his nose at the scent invading the room and downed a beer as he swiped a slice of deluxe pizza from the box.

Eden drank the last of the beer in the bowl and curled up on the couch. At some point Marron joined it. He spoke of the politics surrounding the alliance with

Phrygia and Asgard. He bounced his leg as he explained working with Thor and Freya was easy, but Loki made everything a challenge. Eden tried to listen but lost the battle to its heavy eyes. It must have been drunk because the being curled against the male and slept against his warmth.

CHAPTER 3

Eden awoke the next morning with a pounding headache and cabin fever. Judging by the overall lack of commotion, Meraena and Evan were still asleep in her bedroom. Surprisingly, prince Marron was still sound asleep next to Eden on the couch. It nudged him with her paw. Marron grumbled incoherently and threw his massive arm over his eyes.

Eden sighed and hopped off the couch, eager to find any way out of the apartment. If she could only speak, she would curse the gods for keeping all the doors and windows closed.

Deciding to forego manners, Eden jumped into Marron's lap and batted his cheek with its paw, ignoring the chafe of his stubble against the pad of her foot.

"What?" He groaned; his voice still overtaken by sleep.

Eden bared her teeth, jumped down and ran to the door. She sat down and looked at the handle expectantly.

"Do I have to go with you?" Marron grumbled as he stumbled towards the door, clearly still drunk.

Eden huffed and waited, coiled tail swishing curtly on the cold floor.

Marron opened the door and watched Eden burst out of the apartment, desperate for fresh air. It hoped a change in scenery would be the answer to finding enough peace to shift. Eden knew something vital depended on it, but the understanding of how was still lost to the beast. What had been lost from its memory?

Eden ran with nowhere particular in mind. It stopped when it reached a park full of families playing and laughing. It all felt foreign. Would it ever escape its animal form? Had that ever been its life? Did it even have a family?

A small boy, maybe seven years old, came up to Eden and offered a plucked wildflower to the creature with a smile. His light blue eyes studied the being with great interest. Eden bowed its head to the child.

"Black, to green." The child cocked his head and smiled at Eden. "You'll be okay."

He skipped back to the jungle gym without a care in the world, leaving Eden to consider his statement.

The being craned its head and sniffed the flower. It smelled like hope.

"There you are." Marron sounded out of breath as he jogged to Eden's side. "I couldn't figure out what to do. Would you have known how to get back?"

Eden rolled its eyes at the prince, picked the flower up with its teeth, and jumped up onto a cold metal bench.

"Sometimes I forget that people live lives like this. That parents take their children to the park, and they are free to laugh and play." His flame red hair was in a state of distress from the run. The prince's freckles popped around the flush in his cheeks. "Phrygia, Mt. Olympus, and Asgard all signed a peace treaty fifty years after the one with the humans. I don't know how familiar you are with politics. But this beautiful harmony of fae, humans, demigods, gods, here in Scynthia, …it gives me hope." He leaned back against the park bench, extending his long arms against the cool metal.

Eden gazed at the prince. His attention was still on the children laughing, tumbling on the playground.

"I'm sorry you didn't shift last night. I hope you slept well, though." He glanced down at Eden, who was busy studying its multifaceted form. "I think you need to find a peaceful setting, physically and mentally, before you begin to shift. Whatever is holding you back in this form is likely a mental barrier of yours."

Eden didn't know where or how to achieve that. It dropped the flower and stared at its purple and yellow petals. What would it know of peace?

"Come on, Meraena is surely awake by now. She's probably getting worried." Marron scooped Eden up in his arm as if it were weightless. He grabbed its flower in his other hand and began the journey back to Meraena's apartment.

Eden squirmed in his arms uncomfortably, uneasy with the close embrace.

"Please." He chuckled, looking down at it with sparkling blue eyes. "I watched you try to run. Carrying you is much faster."

Eden grumbled contemptuously.

Marron laughed, but they both knew he was right. They were back at the apartment in short time. *Damn the prince and his long legs,* Eden thought. If only Eden could finally progress and shift, if only it could move forward without help. Eden wanted to scream at whichever god was responsible for its condition in frustration.

Maybe I only have myself to blame. Maybe I had done something truly terrible and was cursed to this form, Eden thought.

Marron set the being down once they arrived in the apartment. They were greeted at the door by a very bubbly Meraena.

"There's fresh coffee in the pot. Evan and I are going to Asgard since the berserkers have trials coming up for graduation. Evan is responsible for training the recruits after his profound success in the war between realms. Eden, do you want to come along?"

Eden looked at everyone in the room. Was she *worthy* of going to the Asgard training fields? To be around these great beings who could shift into rage filled monsters on whim, it seemed to be a joke to put a defect near them. Evan seemed to read its hesitation.

"You are welcome to join us. Maybe meeting other shifters will help you find your form. Marron, you gonna come?" Evan lifted a brow in a subtle dare to the prince.

"I miss those fields." Marron ran a hand over the back of his neck and looked down at Eden with a sigh. "I can't. I've got a rehearsal dinner to plan. Besides, Midas' health has been failing lately. I need to get back."

"Well, if you get bored of that nonsense, come spar with us." Meraena practically danced over to Evan's side and threw an arm around his waist. "The Valkyries and I have some hunting to do today."

Evan kissed the top of his tiny mate's curls and glanced at Eden. "The Valkyries train in the fields next to the berserkers. You'll have a chance to see both major warriors in Asgard. Maybe one will resonate with you." He offered a kind smile. "Shall I carry you, or Meraena?"

Marron grimaced at the offer, shook his head,

and walked out of the room.

"What have you done to the prince, Eden?" Meraena laughed and picked up the creature. "To Asgard!"

CHAPTER 4

With that, the trio departed to an open and vibrantly green mountain landscape. Eden felt as though time slowed down. The world was welcoming her home. The crisp mountain air sang through her lungs. Something about this felt entirely right. The sprites dancing in the sunlight all but lured the being forward.

They entered beyond the large wooden gates and arrived at a fork in the path. To the right, shifters and berserkers could join a large circular fenced ring, where nearly fifty berserkers roared with life and challenged each other to combat. The left fork in the road led to the Valkyries. Their swords could be heard ringing from where Eden, Evan and Meraena stood. Every bone in Eden's body wanted to run towards the Valkyries.

Meraena set Eden down. The creature took in the lush grass caressing its paws. Cool autumn wind cascaded through the mountain-a siren's song of a home long since lost. The plush earth beneath its feet- a welcome mat beckoning the beings arrival. Eden thought that if given the choice, it may never leave.

"Come on." Meraena smiled down at the creature and walked into the Valkyrie camp. Grand white and gold tents lined the rope fence. The smell of the blacksmith's tent consumed the entrance. Valkyries were renowned for their spell cast blades.

"Brynhildr!" Meraena shouted towards the ruby red tent to their left. "I hear you have someone who needs my special interrogation skills?" Long fangs extended from Meraena's gums, dripping with venom.

Eden stared in horror. So Meraena was more than just a mermaid, she was a siren as well.

A tall bronze-skinned woman emerged from the central tent, her long white braid swaying around her black feathered wings with each of her movements. "Ah, yes! I was wondering when you would show up." Her eyes caught Eden. "Welcome, child."

Eden tilted its head.

"In time, dear. In time. For now, welcome to Asgard. I am the leader of the Valkyries." Brynhildr patted the creature's head and ushered Meraena to the barracks behind the Valkyrie sparring ring.

Eden took that to mean that it was not invited. It meandered curiously around the camp and eventually landed on the edge of the berserker ring. Evan was giving orders to beings the resembled something between a bear and a man. Huge claws extended from these beasts' hands. The berserker bodies easily doubled that of their fae forms. Their top half more beast than fae. However, from the waist down their physique was enhanced in muscle but resembled their original body.

Evan was explaining how to use one's body to overpower the enemy, gesturing to weak points on every fae, and why they had to work past the desire to kill first and ask questions later. He was teaching the pups strategy. If they wanted to be seen as soldiers and not maniacs, they would have to fight with method.

A white furred berserker matched with a brown opponent entered the ring, snarling heinously at each other. Saliva spilled from their jowls.

"Stop. Think. Practice our steps." Evan stood between them for a moment before rushing back, allowing the beasts to spar.

If there was a method to the attack, Eden didn't see it. The berserkers in the ring seemed set on murdering one another. The huge white beast drew blood first.

Evan shifted into a beast far more frightening than the growling crew surrounding the ring. "Enough!" He roared. "Shift back now!"

Hesitantly, the two shifted to their fae bodies. Eden was shocked to discover they were no older than teenagers. The white furred one was a female with striking blonde locks, the other a panting male with shaggy brown hair.

Evan shifted as well before declaring to the group, "You will not pass your trials if every blow you land could kill. We know you can kill. The question is, can you control your beast?"

Eden was listening to Evan's lecture when it was startled by a shout from a rotund male next to the being.

"Good gods, what is that thing?" he sneered, pointing at Eden. "Did a berserker get stuck trying to shift?"

Evan leveled him with a solid right hook to the jaw. "Everyone, shift back!" The ring of authority in his voice vibrated through Eden's bones, compelling even her to try and shift.

Hundreds of berserkers shifted back to their fae form and stood at attention at once. Eden thought there must have been some kind of spell cast over the ring, as every one of the berserkers was now back in their uniform. Maintaining clothing was usually a spell wound in the blood of shifters of high fae. The berserkers couldn't all be high fae. Shifters weren't confined to such blood lines.

"Eden is under Meraena's and my protection. Any snide or disrespectful remarks will land you on latrine duty for the next six months. Are we clear?"

"Yes, General," the group chorused.

Evan gazed at Eden sympathetically. "Any one of us could get stuck like them one day. That is the risk of overextending oneself in battle. We are warned from the time we are pups, but few of you seem to comprehend this as a reality."

Everyone grew silent, taking in the truth of Eden. The creature bared its teeth, daring them to pity it, fighting the true urge to find a hole and hide. It didn't want the attention of all the berserkers. All Eden wanted was to find what its true form was.

"Return to your stations." The command was final. Evan stared down the ignorant soldier as he rubbed his jaw and returned to the sparring practice.

Evan returned to training the recruits when a horrifying scream sounded from the Valkyrie camp and a proud smile found Evan's face. "Meraena must be having some fun today." His gaze landed on Eden, a frown creasing his brow. "I wonder if seeing them shift has helped you. I want you to picture the malamute that you want to shift into. Can you do that?"

Eden nodded as she visualized the white and gray canine whose form seemed to embody happiness.

"Good. Now, focus on your breathing." Evan sat on the ground beside her. "Drown out all the sounds around you and lose yourself in your breathing and heartbeat."

Eden closed its eyes and took a deep breath,

filling its lungs with hot summer air. It counted each breath in, sensing the steady thud of its beating heart.

"Good." Evan's voice was growing distant now. "Now, command your body to change to model a malamute."

Eden tried its best. Its eyebrows furrowed as it focused all its energy on the shift, begging every limb and hair to become something else, but was met with utter silence. The universe seemed to mock the beast. Eden let out a defeated snarl, which was rather pathetic considering whatever thing it was had the voice of a tiny kitten.

Evan patted its head. "Give it time. None of us shifted immediately."

Eden dropped onto the too soft and welcoming grass.

Hours passed by. Eden observed the berserkers shifting back and forth from fae bodies to beast forms. They made it look easy. Eventually, Meraena returned with dried blood staining her mouth. Still, she seemed renewed, lively. Evan grinned at the terrifying woman who now entered his ring.

"Well, Eden, shall we go home, shower and order Chinese?"

Eden had no clue if it liked Chinese food, but a shower for Meraena seemed to be a definite necessity. The Creature stood and walked carefully towards the mermaid.

"I will not harm you, Eden. Someday, I'll explain everything, but tonight I am exhausted and hungry." Meraena picked up Eden and blew a kiss back to Evan.

"See you at home." Evan called out as he watched a sparring match between two young berserkers trying to master their rage.

Meraena faded them back to the apartment. She shuffled towards the bathroom mumbling about a shower and grabbed her cellphone to order take out on the way.

Eden jumped onto the couch and huffed. It wanted to roar and destroy something – anything – beyond recognition. Eden's chest ached with that emptiness and need for a life it felt it would never have. It wanted to maul something to death so that by the time it was done Eden would return looking as vengeful and proud as Meraena did.

Meraena entered the room in an oversized hoodie that read "slay enemies and sleep all day" with a mermaid sleeping under a pile of blankets drenched in blood. Eden wished it could laugh aloud. Meraena's hair was wrapped in a purple towel, and she looked refreshed.

Eden couldn't help the jealous pang that rattled its chest. Would slaughtering an enemy bring it contentment?

"Food will be here in twenty." Meraena sat next to Eden. "And surprisingly, so will Marron."

Eden looked at the mer and tilted its head.

"He never visits this much." Meraena frowned as the prince faded into the living room. He had clearly been drinking for quite some time.

"You!" He pointed at Eden. "Why do I feel your emotions? Are you an empath as well as a shifter?" He dropped in front of the creature, alcohol radiating off his breath, stinging Eden's nose. "I am not blood thirsty. I am tired and drunk. Why do I feel you in my mind?"

Marron picked up the creature, who felt much too small in his large arms. "We will be back," he muttered to Meraena before fading.

Marron took them to a grassy field where the blowing wind pushed over the blades of grass. Stars and moonlight shone bright on the valley. The crisp mountain air tickled Eden's nose.

"According to the hawk shifters that work for me, there are thousands of mice here. Go hunt." Marron threw back the last of the contents from the bottle and set Eden down.

Eden stared at the prince in shock for a moment before it heard the telltale scurry of mice. It allowed the long grass to caress its ears as it sunk low to the ground listening for the soft sound. Marron was not wrong; the field was brimming with them. Eden let go of all its inhibitions and stalked its first prey, silently weaving through the weeds, body lowered to the ground crawling. As it snuck up behind the rodent, Eden pounced with all its might. The mouse didn't stand a chance. Blood-tinged Eden's mouth, the bitter copper flavor flooding its senses. Part of it delighted in the rodent's terrified squeals. It needed this. Some part of the beast needed this hunt. Marron waited until Eden sauntered back, proud and sated.

"Thank gods. I hadn't felt that kind of frustration in years." Marron sighed as the bloodlust left Eden's mind. He picked Eden up and returned them to the apartment.

"Ah, I see." Meraena nodded. "Let's get you cleaned up."

Marron settled himself upon the couch as Meraena bathed Eden. Evan faded into the apartment shortly after and joined Marron on the couch to rant about the young berserkers.

Once Eden was dried, they all dived into the Chinese food. Eden loved every bit of it, especially General Tso's.

"Are you staying here?" Meraena asked Marron as she and Evan turned to her room.

"I'll probably hang out on the couch for a while." He stared at the T.V.

"Alright. Goodnight you two." Meraena waved back as Evan ushered them to her room, closing the door gently behind them.

They sat in silence, absently watching humans play football on the T.V. when Marron cleared his throat. "I am sorry for what you are feeling." Marron didn't make eye contact as he continued. "I understand the feeling of being alone and filled with rage you can't do anything about. That doesn't really help you, I know. But you are safe here. All three of us have been in situations where we had to rely on others to get through. It's ok to need us, to need help."

Eden huffed in frustration and pawed at its ears.

"You *will* shift. I know you will." Marron' met Eden's. His sincerity surprised the creature. It curled in a ball on the couch next to Marron and watched the game until the weight of the day finally took its toll.

CHAPTER 5

Eden slept soundly until its slumber was interrupted by a chorus of "whoops" and "hell yeahs" echoing through the apartment. Startled, Eden fell off the couch onto four massive furry paws. The creature looked around with clear eyes.

Marron looked at Eden with eyes brimming with pride. "There you are pup!"

Meraena rushed over and wrapped her arms around Eden in an embrace. "You did it! Even if you were asleep while you did!"

Eden pranced around the room in joy, but it paused as it caught a strange look in Evan's violet eyes. Caution. Fear.

Eden settled at Evan's feet and waited.

"Your aura… I know who you are." Evan ran a hand through his hair, concern shading his eyes. "You're not ready. I swear that when you are, I will be by your side, until the very end. You have my blood oath." Evan unsheathed the sword Eden had failed to notice, from his back, and dropped to his knee. "When you are ready, I am yours."

Meraena frowned and placed a hand on his shoulder, staring at Eden. "I don't know who you are, but if Evan will, then you have my loyalty as well."

Marron took a step back, looking between Evan and Eden. "Who is it?"

Evan looked at Eden. "To tell you, would be to betray an entire kingdom. War will come when the truth is revealed."

Eden's ears dropped and its body lowered defensively to the floor. Marron placed a hand gently on its head. "Fuck's sake, Evan. The thing just shifted for the first time in gods knows how long-"

"Two hundred years. It has been stuck in this form for two hundred years." Evan laid a gentle hand on Eden, meeting its eyes with sympathy. "Bravery, courage and bad-assery like none other are all words that define you, Eden. You may have forgotten, but your people, the realm you saved, they remember."

"Eden has been stuck in that form for two hundred years?" Meraena asked.

"No, Eden has been missing for two hundred

years." Evan watched Marron, whose hand had yet to leave Eden's head.

Marron was the first to ask, "How do you know who it is?"

"The scent, now that it is one being. Also, its aura changed, which for now is as much on that as I can share. The aura is likely what will cause the war." Evan peered down at the animal. "You, my friend, are in good company and will always have a home in Asgard. Meraena, I have to return to my troops. Are you coming with me this time, or staying here?"

Meraena looked at Eden. "What do you think?"

Eden didn't know what to think. In fact, it almost wanted to lean into Marron who had gone uncharacteristically quiet.

It peered at the prince who was rubbing his chest and frowning. "I need to go home before Midas throws a fit. I'll see you all around." With that, the prince grabbed the last beer and left.

Asgard it was.

Meraena pulled her beautiful purple curls into a tight bun atop her head. She dressed in fighting leathers, which Eden had to admit was a stark contrast to her typical floral and colorful palette. This version of Meraena would make any enemy think twice before crossing her path.

"Will others in Asgard know who Eden is now that it's shifted?" Meraena asked Evan as they locked her apartment door.

"Undoubtedly. There are markings in its aura that cannot be hidden from us. However, Eden is not Asgard's enemy. If anything, we could be an ally to it."

Eden looked up at Evan. That was quite a declaration to make in a realm with gods as fickle as Zeus.

Evan chuckled as if reading her mind and draped an arm around his mate. "No one knows the mind of Odin, but I can guarantee Freya, Loki, Thor, and Hel will guard you."

"Poseidon, my father. Would he guard her?" Meraena grabbed his hand and searched his eyes for honesty.

"I don't know," the berserker's brow furrowed as he assessed her question. "The Olympians are the unpredictable ones in Eden's case." He placed a kiss upon her forehead, then said with a wicked grin, "Ready to make those Norse trainees throw up?"

Meraena shook her head and smiled despite herself. She placed a hand on Eden. Evan nodded and that was all it took before they were faded to Asgard.

The golden gate opened immediately for Evan. Eden expected some attention after Evan's declaration, but it was unprepared for the stares from wildlife. A faun glanced at the malamute before taking a knee, just as Evan had. Eden suddenly wished it had followed Marron to wherever he had gone.

Meraena laid a hand on Eden's shoulder and followed Evan toward the training fields.

Evan glanced around at the fire sprites gathered around the walking path. He cleared his throat and addressed their presence. "I know who you see with us, but for now they go by Eden. Help us inform those who need to know. Eden's safety is our priority at this time."

The sprites flashed brightly in unison before vanishing altogether. Evan pulled his dark brown hair into a bun similar to Meraena's revealing an elegant tattoo of Yggdrasil on the base of his neck. Meraena held his hand until they reached what Eden assumed must be the barracks.

The dog sat and assessed Asgard. There was a tugging feeling in the being's chest that it could not ignore. The creatures around it screamed with familiarity, but Eden couldn't conclude if that meant it was in danger. Evan seemed to think Asgard would be loyal to it, but to what end? And for what purpose?

Padded moss grew around Eden forming the softest of beds the being had ever rested upon in nature. Eden looked down and pawed the plant gently in its best attempts in a thank you.

Woodland sprites danced around twinkling in their acceptance of it and flew around the dog's face. One bright blue sprite offered the dog a day lily with a lavender starburst center. Eden bowed its head to the sprites. Why were the sprites offering the being such kindness? Did Eden even deserve it?

Meraena watched the procession with avid curiosity but met with the Valkyries and began sword work immediately. The woman was lethal, as she met each attack with precision. Her sword sang with each strike. Several moments passed before her opponent was on the ground surrendering.

Hours passed and Eden eventually meandered into the barracks, following the scent of Evan and the other berserkers. Eden struggled to find him in his shifted form, but eventually found a huge berserker bearing Evan's sword, leading several pups through counter-attack measures. Eden had the common sense to remain a good distance from the beasts with feral instincts. The being was met with several wary glances as it watched the soldiers prepare.

Without warning, the skies darkened, and thunder shook the ground, lightning striking the mountain tops. All training stopped and warriors fell silent. A god was coming.

From the storm raking the skies, Eden expected Thor. The berserkers stood at attention as Loki simply appeared in the center of the training ring. He was clad in emerald-green fighting leathers. His ocean blue eyes glowed. A berserker, still in beast form, lost control of its rage and charged the god. Loki tossed it effortlessly onto its back.

"Eden." He crouched down to eye level with the being. "The sprites informed me of our guest." As he stood, Loki cleared his throat and looked at the berserker walking towards him.

Evan shifted back to his fae form, chest exposed, still panting from training. "Eden is unaware of what or who he or she is. Its aura reveals he or she is not ready to learn the truth yet. It will break its mind."

Loki's jaw clenched. "Come here, Eden."

Eden stood and walked towards the God of fire and mischief. It resolved not to shake in fear.

I am not afraid, the being repeated this until it stood toe to toe with Loki.

"You live." Eden wasn't sure if that was a statement or question. He held either side of Eden's face tenderly. "This is not over. We will rain destruction on their kingdom as soon as you are ready."

Eden met Loki's sky-blue gaze and saw the fire burning within. Whatever he was referencing, his oath was binding. Eden could not make sense of why everyone was making promises to it but bowed its head in acceptance.

Meraena appeared at Eden's side and Loki assessed her.

"Hmm. I suppose a trip to Olympus could bring a unique turn of events to the situation at hand." He rubbed his jaw and turned to Evan. "Eden, I understand this must be a shock, but you have a room in my house from your past. Should you need or want it, I will be sure accommodations are prepared. I want to be alerted the moment Eden is ready to begin this war. This is Eden's decision and will be the entire way through."

What war is everyone talking about, Eden wondered as Loki glanced at Meraena.

Evan nodded and saluted the god. Eden wasn't sure the comments it heard leave Loki's mouth fit what it knew to be true of the mischievous lord.

Meraena looked to Evan. "Eden is…?"

"Yes." Evan crossed his muscled arms, his violet eyes tenderly looking down at Eden.

Eden was growing tired of the pitying looks. It growled its displeasure at Evan.

He chuckled and nodded. "There you are. Very well. You don't deserve pity. You deserve revenge."

"Revenge is what we all shall have," Loki remarked, venom coating every word. "Come to my home this evening, General. I would honor you and your mate for returning Eden to Asgard."

Evan exchanged a look with Meraena.

She looked down at Eden. "I need to return to my shores in two days, but one night will be okay."

Loki simply snapped his fingers and suddenly the lot of them were inside a black marble castle, gold veins flowing through the walls and floor. A huge fireplace roared in the grand living area where dark golden leather sofas adorned the space. Eden wasn't sure what compelled it to beeline to the fireplace. It took a deep breath and inhaled the smell of nutmeg, dark chocolate, and orange zest. Home. The tugging in Eden's chest intensified and the being let out a soft whimper.

Loki immediately rushed to its side and placed a tender hand on its shoulder. "We read many books in this corner for years, my dear. You are home."

Tears ran down the creature's cheeks and wet its fur.

"Honey. I was preparing a roast for dinner, and I thought I heard a commotion. Do we have guests?" A redheaded woman in an emerald gown entered the living room. She fell to her knees in a choked sob when she met Eden's eyes.

Loki smiled tenderly at the woman and left Eden's side. "Angrboda, this is Eden. Eden, this is my wife. General Evan and his mate Meraena brought her to the barracks today during training. The sprites brought word of Eden to Thor and I."

"She's home." Angrboda wept into the fair, freckled-covered hands covering her mouth.

She. Eden was a woman. The dog looked toward Meraena and Evan for confirmation. They both nodded. Meraena's eyes were brimming with tears. Who was she to Loki and Angrboda? Eden tried to remember what she knew of the Norse lineage, but there was a barrier-blocking her from her past. It was as if there was a physical wall blocking her memories.

Evan cleared his throat. "Angrboda, we know

this was unexpected. Meraena and I can give you all time as a family if you need it."

Eden's heart raced at the thought of being abandoned. Even if this once used to be her home, it still felt bad. She stomped her paw and Loki laughed.

"Oh, she's there all right. General, you two aren't going anywhere. I know that stance and she isn't letting you leave her side without a fight. We may be familiar to her, but we are still strangers."

Meraena got on the floor next to Eden, making eye contact. "Loki, while not always my first choice of allies – no offense –" The god shrugged and picked a piece of lint from his top. "Marron had mentioned you were looking for something tirelessly. It was this! *Her.*"

Loki nodded in confirmation. His eyes remained on Eden as she took everything in.

Meraena continued. "I know little of your upbringing. That would be Evan's area of expertise, but if you want me to stay tonight, I will. You may also stay as my roommate in Scynthia when I return."

Eden nuzzled Meraena and Angrboda reached out towards them.

"May I please? May I touch you?" Angrboda asked. Eden wondered why she sounded so hesitant when Loki hadn't. Was it his arrogance, or was it deeper than that?

Eden bowed her head and Angrboda caressed the malamute's cheek. Every stroke seemed to scream mother. A gentle caress that one would give to their young child. Eden pressed her head to Angrboda's chest and whined.

"My sweet child." Angrboda held the dog in her lap. Loki motioned for Evan to follow him down a candle-lit hallway. Meraena nodded to him as he left. She certainly hadn't realized saving a stray shifter would bring about such a change in their fate.

Meraena kept a healthy distance as mother and daughter reunited, though she expected an entirely different reunion when Eden found her fae form again. The separation between Loki, Angrboda, and Eden was remembered as cataclysmic.

"I will escort you two to the guest wing. I assume you and your mate wish to share a room?" Angrboda, still embracing Eden, asked Meraena.

"Yes, that would be lovely. Thank you." Meraena smiled politely, glancing at Eden. If the knowledge of who she was and what happened to her could break her mind, was returning to her childhood home too much too soon? Eden stepped back from Angrboda glancing between Meraena and her mother.

She nudged Meraena's hand, sensing her unease. She offered her a gentle smile. "This is a lot to *me*. I worry about you."

Eden leaned fully into Meraena as Angrboda spoke quietly to a maid who appeared seemingly from thin air.

"This is Sophia. She has been here for centuries and knows the castle well. She will take you to your rooms while I finish dinner."

Sophia was likely a fire fae, judging by the way her long sleek onyx hair seemed to emit sparks with each of her swaying steps. She guided Eden and Meraena to a grand spiraling staircase behind the living room. Lined with candlelit sconces, the black and gold marble continued throughout the stairwell and hallway they landed upon. Yet a lush seafoam teal carpet lining the corridor on this hallway padded their feet. Eden and Meraena stared at one another at the contrast.

Sophia laughed. "This is the princess' level. When you were about twenty years old you designed the rooms and color choices. If I recall, there was a very loud debate between you and Loki about not everything needing to be 'doom and gloom all the time.'"

Meraena laughed. "I cannot wait to hear these stories from you, Eden."

Eden pawed the vibrant carpet and continued following the maid.

Sophia stopped before the first door on the right. The door was covered in ornate ivy and blooming day lilies, just the same as those that were presented to her at the training fields that morning. "This is of course your room, Eden."

Eden stared at the door for a long moment. Sophia turned to open the door, but Eden blocked the movement with her body.

"I am so exhausted from training today. Can you show me my room? I would love to freshen up before dinner." Meraena smiled at Sophia politely.

The maid recovered quickly and nodded, escorting them down the hall to the neighboring room. Its door was made of solid chestnut with golden door fixtures. A simple guest room entrance compared to Eden's.

"Thank you, Sophia. We appreciate your time."

Sophia offered a curtsy before leaving. Meraena blew a long breath out. "Your dad is Loki. You are your own being. We have so much to discuss whenever you're ready. I think that when that day comes, we'll prepare a proper rage room at home and get good and properly drunk, maybe high. Whatever you want babe, we are going to make it happen."

Eden felt honesty through her friend's words. Meraena opened the door to a bright room with a gigantic golden bed covered in a white downy comforter. A granite fireplace was blazing in the corner with a bear fur rug strewn on the floor in front of it. A large bay window overlooked the mountains and ocean.

"Not the worst guest room." Meraena smiled at Eden. "You are welcome to stay here with me tonight. Evan has a room in the barracks."

Eden laid on the fireplace rug, which earned a chuckle from Meraena. "Alright, I will let him know."

Eden huffed.

"I don't know what that means. Evan?"

Eden nodded.

"Wouldn't it be weird if we all stayed in the same room?"

Eden made a great show of turning her back on Meraena and closing her eyes.

Meraena laughed. "We can discuss that with him."

A deep familiar voice came from the doorway, "Discuss what with him?"

Meraena shook her head at Evan and ran her fingers through the waves that had formed in his hair as a result of wearing it up in a bun all day. "Would you mind Eden staying in our room this evening? She isn't ready to go to her old room yet."

Evan popped Meraena's hair out of its ponytail and ruffled her curls as well. "Eden, you are most welcome to stay, but I am not leaving my mate in your father's home unguarded. So yes, we will all have to be roomies for the night."

Eden chuffed an agreement. Loki and Angrboda played the parts of doting parents well, but Eden wasn't sure that that was the full story. She nudged Evan's hand and grunted.

Evan looked at Meraena. "I don't know what that means…"

"You have to try." Meraena laughed. "Loki? Evan's meeting with Loki?"

Eden nodded.

Meraena gestured at Eden. "See? Just ask."

Evan kissed her cheek. "I will explain fully when we go home. For now, we are safe. Loki does love you and Asgard loves you. Your loss was devastating to everyone here. However, remember that Loki gets off on mischief and discord and operates accordingly. You just made his century both for the fact that he loves you, and for the fact that your return guarantees war and chaos. I believe waiting until you have your memory back is best before explaining further. You are so close to shifting. I can see it in the strengthening of your aura."

Eden listened intently to the general and took in all the information, still confused by war seemed to follow her.

"Even after my three centuries in service to the Asgardian army, I know as much as you do about Angrboda. I feel like we can trust her, but that is more from watching her aura react to your return than from my direct contact with her. She is a very quiet woman, but that is not to say she is passive. I do not believe Loki would thrive with a subservient wife."

A soft knock sounded on the door.

"Dinner is ready." Sophia announced.

"I could definitely eat." Meraena clutched her stomach. "And drink. Gods, I hope Angrboda serves wine with her meals."

"Your priorities are always perfectly right, my dear." Evan kissed the top of her head before opening the door. "Think politics. Remain calm. Above all else, stay neutral, even if you feel ready to explode."

Good lords, Eden hoped it wouldn't come to that.

The trio arrived at the dining room, where they

were seated by a white granite expanse of a table. Loki sat at the end with Angrboda to his right. The arrangements felt odd, forced. A roast, potatoes and several bottles of wine adorned the center of the table.

"Thank you for having us, Angrboda. Dinner looks absolutely stunning."

"You are most welcome. Thank you for returning our daughter. It is a debt that will not be forgotten. Please, eat."

Meraena opened her mouth to object, but Evan placed a hand on hers. "Thank you so much," he said. "I am famished. Those berserker pups are feral."

"Hm." Loki was watching Eden with intent. "I have heard the new generations are something to watch for sure."

Meraena filled a plate and placed it on the floor in front of Eden. Evan and Meraena filled their own as Loki continued to stare at Eden.

"Dear," Angrboda began, placing a tender – or was it timid? – hand on Loki's knee. "You must be hungry as well. Let us celebrate the joyous day today has become."

Too loudly, and with an abrupt clap of his hands, Loki replied. "Yes, you are correct." He filled a plate with roast and took an enormous bite of meat before speaking around it. "I just know that I raised a fighter. Spell or no spell, I do believe she should be able to withstand the knowledge of her name and understand why she has come into the situation she has."

"This is not the –" Angrboda pleaded, her vibrant green eyes beseeching her partner.

"Now is *exactly* the time. She is home! War planning should begin now, and that starts with breaking the curse Hecate placed on our daughter centuries ago."

"Loki, look at her aura. She is close, yes. She's almost ready to know the truth, but pushing the issue could cause her to permanently be stuck in this form, never to know her true abilities again. It's too much on for her mind right now." Evan, the voice of reason, held the fuming stare of the god of mischief.

Eden was fed up with everyone speaking on her behalf. Dammit, she didn't even know what she was supposed to start a war over but she sure as hell couldn't do it as a dog. Vibrating with anger, Eden raised her hackles and howled. She would do this. She would fight her way to her true form. She certainly didn't need her father and friend's mate arguing over her head. Her limbs continued to vibrate. Heat flared around her, and soon…

Loki stood so fast his chair tipped backwards. "Marvelous!"

"Stop her! We have no clue where she will go," Angrboda shouted.

"What is happening? She is on fire!" Meraena attempted to run towards her friend, but Evan wrapped his arms around her waist.

"This is Fenryn's power. She is fading." Evan watched as their friend disappeared, leaving nothing but smoke and her plate behind.

CHAPTER 6

"Oh my gods!" Marron shouted and jumped on top of his bed at the sudden appearance of a flaming dog in his bedroom. He immediately grabbed for the sheathed sword strapped to his back. His hands failed on the first two attempts – the fae wine from his engagement celebration that night still running strong. At last, he withdrew the blade and wielded it at the blazing ball of fur before him.

Eden's flames died down as she continued her howl from Loki's castle, eyes still closed.

Brows furrowed, Marron dropped his sword on the mattress and wobbled off the mattress. "Eden?"

She blinked and looked at Marron and began barking a long trail of nonsense.

"Eden, I have no clue what's going on, but I am way too drunk to explain to my father's staff what a dog on fire is doing in my room in the middle of the night. You must stop barking." Marron placed a shushing finger on her snout for emphasis.

Eden bared her teeth and growled.

Marron chuckled and flopped into a crossed legged seat next to her. "Where are Meraena and Evan? Do they know where you are?"

Eden looked about the room in panic. She jumped on the prince's bed, ruffling the bedding.

"Excuse me! I don't know where you came from, but it is disrespectful to toss a prince's bed without permission. What the Hel are you-"

Eden pushed his cellphone onto the floor with an unceremonious thunk.

"Oh. Yes, I can text them. Eden appeared in my room on fire. All is well. We are going to keep drinking and go back to the apartment. Sounds good to you?"

Eden studied the prince and wondered if he could manage walking out his bedroom door. Tentatively, she nodded. In the end, what options did she have?

"Wonderful!" His speech was a slurred disaster. His auburn hair fell into his eyes as he reached for his beer bottle. "Let's blow this nightmare!"

Eden sat emphatically and stared at the beer.

"Don't be a buzzkill, Eden. You didn't have to

sit next to Miss Cries Every Ten Minutes and assure her that you won't rape her once the marriage is final. Gods, if there was any loophole to break this cursed engagement I would do it. I can't imagine eternity with a woman who can't laugh or fight. So, no. The emotional support beer stays."

Eden rolled her eyes and stepped aside.

"Nah, we aren't walking out there. We are fading." He placed a hand on her shoulder and suddenly, if not a bit of a rough ride as his inebriation impacted his ability to smoothly fade, they were dumped at the doorstep of Meraena's apartment. "No one besides Meraena and Evan knows that I can do that." Marron brushed the dirt off his slacks as he pulled himself off the ground. "So," he put his hand to her nose again, earning him another annoyed shove. "Gods, I can't wait to meet you, Eden. You're going to be fun. Come on, let's raid the liquor cabinet."

Eden watched the man as he removed his sword from his back – wrestling with the tangled shoulder strap throughout the process – and hung it haphazardly on the coat rack along with his suit jacket. The thin white button-up underneath did nothing to hide Marron's muscular frame and the whirling expanse of tattoos covering his back. Interesting indeed, Eden thought.

"Alright, Eden. I have no clue what kind of liquor you like. So! Let's start with an amaretto sour and build from there. Since you've shifted, your fae genes can probably withstand a drink or two." With clear familiarity with Meraena's apartment, Marron grabbed several bottles from the liquor cabinet, along with cherries, lemons, and tonic from the fridge. He took bowl and his glass from a nearby cabinet and laid them all out on the kitchen island. He unbuttoned his cuffs and rolled his sleeves up, exposing more black ink in a pattern Eden couldn't quite make out. With the finesse of a skilled bartender, Marron measured and poured the liquors into a mixer, then flipped and tossed it through the air. He drained the contents into a crystal bowl he placed at Eden's feet.

"M'lady." He grinned, dimples creasing his tanned cheeks as he placed the drink in front of Eden's snout.

Eden took a sip tentatively. It was delicious! She all but inhaled the drink. Once it was gone, she nudged the bowl back towards him.

Marron laughed and drank his own cocktail. "That's my girl."

Eden sat up abruptly, staring at the prince as he mixed her another drink.

"What? Don't look at me like that. Drink more, stop thinking so much. I believe you're a woman under there. It fits."

Eden rolled her eyes and accepted the bowl as it was returned to her. Marron crossed the kitchen to the living room and turned on the TV. He flipped through the channels until eventually landing on The Princess Bride. "Come on. Let's watch a killer movie and forget the world exists for a few hours."

Eden finished her drink and jumped on the couch, sitting against Marron's opposite arm. He took a long sip of his drink before entering a monologue of Westley's adventures with the Dread Pirate Roberts. "Good night, Westley. Good work. Sleep well. I'll most likely kill you in the morning." Marron recited with an emphatic hand to his chest and the other holding his beer high in the air. Taking a sip from his glass he whispered, "As you wish."

Eden wasn't sure whether to watch Marron or the movie. He grunted and unbuttoned the top two buttons of his shirt. "These actors had the best clothes. I'd wear tunics over fitted suits any day."

Eden chuffed and turned to sit closer to him.

Marron loosed a sigh and threw his head back against the couch. "I want a unified kingdom. I want a wife who will fight wars and sit councils beside me. I want a father who is not fucking Midas. I want to be Westley. Or Inigo Montoya. Both are great."

She placed her paw gently on his knee.

He laid his arm across her gently. "What would you say if you weren't a dog, Eden? Would you pity me? Would there be sass? Who *are* you?"

She wished she could tell him. Wished she knew which pocket his phone was in so she could make him ask Meraena.

"I think you would hand me my ass every day of the week." He laid his head on the back of the couch, closing his eyes.

  Eden wasn't far behind. Her head fell into his lap and the two crashed on the couch to sleep.

CHAPTER 7

Marron was the first to wake to the sound of the front door opening. When he looked down at his lap, he was surprised not to see a dog, but rather a fully-grown beautiful naked woman laying her head there. Black waves of hair cascaded across her ivory shoulders and covered an ungodly number of scars on her back. Scars so long and thick that not even fae should have been able to withstand.

"Who is she?" Marron demanded from Meraena, who rushed towards them with a blanket from the entryway closet.

"How dare you? You're engaged! So, what? The minute she's back to being a human you get her drunk and naked? What have you *done*?" Meraena whispered forcefully as she covered her friend.

"Fuck you," Marron countered, trying to figure out what to do with his hands and the very naked woman sleeping in his lap.

Evan released a warning growl.

"She was a dog when we fell asleep! Who is

she? Who did this? Tell me they are dead." Marron wrapped his arms around Eden, his hold tightening with every passing thought of the torture inflicted upon her.

Eden grunted and tossed in her sleep. Her face revealed a fair skinned beauty, with a striking scar cutting through her left eyebrow.

"That is Loki's daughter, Fenryn. She was married to Apopis. Her story is not mine to tell." Meraena's eyes filled with tears. "But she entered into a deal with Hecate to save her people from her husband. It trapped her in an animal form with no memories for two hundred years and trapped her husband until the spell was broken. I don't know what the conditions were, but her kingdom was evacuated and if she is female again, then I would assume Apopis is not far behind. Evan thought telling her when she wasn't ready would prolong her struggle to shift."

"*Marron*," Evan warned as he observed Marron's sudden change in aura and protectiveness of Fenryn. "Fuck off. Fuck you. Loki?" That explained the god's uneasiness lately. He had been searching for his daughter. Marron raked his hands through his hair and went through what he knew about Fenryn. The lore around her was scant. Hel, she disappeared two hundred years ago. He was 50 years old when she disappeared and gave no fucks about politics. Apopis wasn't anyone he had met or had dealings with. "Who is Apopis?"

Evan shook his head. "He's not someone you fuck around with. He is a god of chaos and demons. Loki arranged the marriage to see what his chaos could look like when mixed with hers."

Rage built in Marron's chest. The scars covering her body screamed of abuse the prince couldn't begin to fathom. Every instinct flowing through the prince demanded he protect Fenryn with his life. He couldn't imagine what devastation Eden – no, Fenryn – would rain once she came to. The princess adjusted in her sleep and laid one arm under her head. Marron took her in, noting the iron-shackle burns wrapped around her wrists. How long had she been held in shackles? What exactly had she done to escape?

"You should probably leave before she wakes up," Meraena whispered. Her gaze caught on the shackle burn as well.

"Like Hel, Meraena. I am not leaving her. We are all part of this now." Marron's eyes never left the woman in his lap.

"Marron, you are not exactly an ally to her father. Asgard's relationship with Phrygia has been rocky ever since your father refused to marry Freya's daughter. Joining an alliance with her, if she chooses to collaborate with her father, could be catastrophic for your position. Your father would lose what's left of his mind."

Marron glared at Evan. The berserker threw his hands up in an apologetic surrender, but he knew he wasn't wrong. Marron and his family had made no effort to broker a peace with the Asgardian gods over the years.

Eden turned, her face resting against Marron's abdomen. He gently tucked her hair behind her ear and simply stared at her.

"I'm making coffee." Meraena blew out a breath. "None of us will survive this morning without it. Evan, go buy doughnuts or bagels or some easy premade food. I foresee Eden losing her shit about being a woman again and we will all need the fuel."

Evan chuckled, offered Meraena a sloppy salute and exited the apartment. Once the door closed, a sock hit Marron's head.

"The Hel, Mer?" He tossed the sock onto the floor.

"You. Are. Engaged." Meraena threw coffee grounds into a filter while glaring at the prince.

"Like you got to choose!" Marron frowned at Eden. "Love means nothing if it's not reciprocated. Judging by the scars and burns on her body, she may very well despise all men and wish to live a life of celibacy, Mer. This isn't even remotely the time to think about it."

"You will have to." Meraena turned to stare out the kitchen window, likely remembering her refusal in the early years with Evan. The fates had chosen Evan as her mate, but Poseidon had his own opinions on his mer daughter being bound to a berserker. It was unheard of.

"I have time." Marron resisted the urge to touch Eden again, and pulled the blanket up to her shoulders, taking in the detailed tattoo branching over her right shoulder. Yggdrasil, he thought, though there was part of the tattoo that carried to her back which hinted at more than the tree of life.

The coffee pot gurgled, and Eden's nose twitched, her eyes slowly opening. Marron's breath caught at the striking emerald gaze. She offered a soft smile to the prince before stretching and exposing her breasts from the blanket.

Marron bit back his laugh and covered his eyes. "Eden…"

"Holy shit!" The woman looked down at her naked body and practically flew off the couch, releasing a harrowing scream.

"Fenryn – Eden –" Meraena started. She slowly approached the naked female who now grasped her midsection and collapsed to the ground in sobbing gasps.

Marron grabbed the throw from the couch and gently placed it back around Eden, sitting next to the two females.

"My people. Please. Gods. My people? Did they

survive?" She didn't lift her head, only stared at the burns on her wrists.

"You got them out, Fenryn. I don't know the entire story, but Hecate offered them amnesty and has protected them ever since." Meraena reached out to place a hand on Fenryn, but the woman pulled back.

"Apopis. If I am awake…"

"We are aware. We will make a game plan, but let's get you dressed first. Evan is on his way back with food."

Marron met Fenryn's stare. Her eyes lit his soul like the fires at the Ostara festivals. He tried to say something, anything, but failed.

The connection Marron felt was irrefutable. Her blood lust he had felt nights prior suddenly made sense. She was his mate. He could feel the undeniable tether of the bond growing in his chest with every passing second near her.

"Fenryn, or Eden?" He finally asked after bobbing his mouth like a fish for far too long.

"Fenryn." She held his gaze, taking in the prince's stare. "I appreciate you offering me the name

Eden, Meraena. Thank you. Thank you for all your kindness."

Fenryn wrapped the blanket around her and stood. She marveled at the plush pink fibers caressing her skin as she held it tight. The throw fell above her knees, exposing burns similar to those on her wrists around her ankles. Marron thought he might be sick from the fury building in his chest.

"You are taller than I am." Meraena smiled up at Fenryn who was, indeed, a solid foot taller than the mermaid. "I don't know what I have that will fit you. Maybe   leggings   and…"

"Let her use one of my tunics in the closet." Evan entered the apartment with a large box of doughnuts in hand. "The perks of a giantess mother." He laughed. "You're, what, 6'3? Meraena, babe, your 5'2 clothes wouldn't do."

Fenryn smirked and tightened the throw around her.

"I just didn't want to throw her in men's clothes on her first day back," Meraena grumbled and took Fenryn to her room.

When the door closed, Evan turned to Marron. "Can you tolerate her in my clothes?"

Marron fumed. "If you weren't mated, I'd likely stick a blade in you for the implication." He sighed. "I do understand, though. I have nothing to offer her here… so, your clothes will be… fine."

Evan tipped his head back and laughed. "You are in so much trouble."

"Don't I know it." Marron grabbed a sprinkle-covered doughnut from the box and took a hearty bite.

After a while of the women rummaging through Evan's stash, Fenryn emerged in a royal blue button-up dress shirt. Fenryn left the first two buttons undone, and the rest loosely buttoned. It hung just below her hips. Black tights hugged her long legs, ending about an inch above her ankles, and damn it, the prince was staring.

"You've got some sprinkles, Marron. Just there." Fenryn gestured to his chin and smirked, offering him a napkin.

Her long black hair, now rested in a fishtail braid which ended at the middle of her back. She reached for a doughnut as Marron swiped at his mouth.

Evan hid his chuckle behind a coffee mug.

Fenryn moaned and rolled her eyes to the back of her head when she took her first bite. "Gods, I forgot how delicious these things are."

Marron nearly choked on the bite in his mouth. He felt a sudden urge to adjust his pants.

Evan clapped him on the shoulder. "Welcome back to the land of the Fae, Fenryn. So, do we want to talk war now or should we wait?"

"Do not speak of war until I have eaten my doughnut and had at *least* half a cup of coffee. I swear to Hades, Evan I will arrange a training session with the entire underworld if you keep me from eating in peace."

Marron laughed. "You had to know better by now, man."

Evan smirked, raising a brow, "Oh yes, but it's so fun to get under her scales."

Meraena growled as she poured her drink. She dropped onto a chair and grabbed a chocolate sprinkle covered confection. "We will see how much you like it when you don't get laid for a week."

That wiped the grin off the berserker's face.

Fenryn had stopped eating and was now watching the interaction between her friends. She waited for Meraena to finish her doughnut before beginning, "I expect no allies. I know Olympus and Asgard are not exactly sympathetic to one another. Evan, I appreciate your pledge of loyalty, though I have to wonder how that will go over with my father. He will want every part of this battle. If I can avoid it, though, there will be no war."

Marron stopped drinking his coffee and slammed his mug to the table. "Are you going to let that monster go?"

Fenryn's eyes lit, two glowing embers. "His death will be at my hands, but I will not ask for anyone to sacrifice their lives in this endeavor. Enough have perished by Apopis' hands."

Meraena shot Marron a warning glance. "We may not be armed with forces like our parents, but if you will have us, Evan and I will help you in any way we can. I work with the Valkyries often, and I know they will aid you too. Evan and the berserkers, well, berserkers are always ready for a good fight."

"You don't know what you are up against." Fenryn rubbed her wrists.

"No," Marron agreed, meeting her gaze. "But we sure as hell won't let you face it alone."

Fenryn studied him, then took in the sincerity of Meraena and Evan. "I need to return to Asgard. I need my weapons. I need to train. Gods, it's been too long. I don't even know what powers I have left. I –"

Marron laid a hand on hers, barely a whisper of a touch. "I will train you."

"So will the berserkers and the Valkyries." Evan nodded. "We will not venture into this unprepared."

Fenryn withdrew her hand from Marron's and stood. "Meraena, you said you had to return to the seas today. I am going to gather some things from Asgard, may I return to the apartment when finished?"

"Of course. You may stay in the guest room." Meraena finished the last drop of coffee, tipping her head back as far as she could, then stood. "I have to go. I'll be home in two days. Um, Evan. Can you set her up with a phone and put my number in it?"

"Wait. Just wait." Marron held up a hand. "Who

is going to Asgard with you?"

"I do not need anyone to go with me, *prince.*" Fenryn glared. "It is my birthplace. I will be safe."

"Will you? Your family didn't protect you from Apopis, and you expect everyone will just welcome you back? What of Apopis? The first place he will look for you will be your home!"

"I am well aware, and I know how to remain hidden." Fenryn crossed her arms and fought back the urge to assert her dominance over the man.

"Great. Then stay hidden with me." Marron mirrored her pose. "Two hundred years is a long time without access to your powers. Hel, you just shifted in your sleep! You don't even remember how to shift intentionally. Both times you did, you were either drunk or asleep."

Smoke escaped Fenryn's fingertips. Meraena looked between the two and shook her head. "Right, you guys figure that out. Babe, I'll see you Friday. I love you."

Evan kissed his mate goodbye, chuckling at the battle taking place at the breakfast table. "Love you."

Meraena left in a blink, leaving Fenryn with the two men, one grinning ear to ear, while the other was about to lose his mind.

"Don't you have a fiancé that needs you?" Fenryn taunted, narrowing her eyes.

"Don't you think this is more important?"

Evan shook his head. "You two are going to be fun. How about we *all* go since I'm training the recruits everyday anyway."

Fenryn slowly shifted her gaze away from Marron. "I can agree to that. I think the barracks will be good enough for getting weapons. I *will* begin training today."

"Then we will train with you." Marron stood.

Fenryn glared and crossed her arms.

Evan assessed the situation before nodding. "Alright, let's go."

CHAPTER 8

Fenryn was ready to tear Marron to shreds. Like Hel did she need a man playing protector. She was nothing to him! He had no right to be so concerned.

The trio landed outside the barracks and walked to the armory. Evan gestured for Marron to follow him as Fenryn spoke with the blacksmith.

Fenryn squared her shoulders as she approached the tent. She was fae again. The daughter of Loki. She belonged here. The hesitation weighing down her chest was unnecessary, yet it stayed.

"I knew it." The smith wiped her brow, smearing soot across her ash covered forehead. Her pale brown eyes brimmed with tears. "You came back. You're alive. There is hope."

Fenryn rubbed her wrists, looking away for a moment. "I…um. Thank you, but I need weapons and training before I can even dream of being worthy of the look in your eye."

The smith wiped her hands on her apron and took Fenryn's in hers. "What you sacrificed for us, what you did to yourself to protect us…you are worthy just as you are. Thank you. You saved me and my infant brother all those years ago. I made these about a year ago in honor of your name day. I never knew I would be able to present them to you one day."

She reached beneath her booth and pulled out an elegant wooden box, covered in lilies and vines.

Fenryn held herself back and fought the knot forming in her throat. The blacksmith opened the box and revealed the most exquisite sword and dagger set Fenryn had ever set eyes on. The knot work around emeralds placed in the hilts took her breath away.

"They will respond to your fire. When you unleash it, the blades will become an extension of you. Bring that beast to his knees."

"I will, and when I do, it will be your blades that fell him. Thank you. I need to return to my father's estate before I can pay you."

"I will not accept it." The smithy smiled. "You have earned them. They are yours."

"Give me your name then, so I may honor your reputation." Fenryn ran her fingers over the sword's scabbard.

"Aleya Johansen." The female smiled with pride, dimples taking over her freckle covered cheeks. "Now go show that grumbling man what Fenryn, daughter of Loki, is capable of."

She turned around to see Marron, indeed, was watching their interaction. A saccharine smile took over her face. "I look forward to doing just that, but I can't fight in these clothes." She frowned at the dress shirt. It would be torn to shreds instantly.

"The Valkyries may have leathers that will fit." Aleya, the blacksmith, pointed to the Valkyrie training field. "Calliope should be able to help you."

"Thank you, Aleya." Fenryn tied the sword across her back and slid the dagger into the waist of her pants before sauntering over to Marron.

"If you are going to glare at my back all day, you may as well do so by my side."

Marron blinked at her. "I wasn't – it's not – damn it, I don't like this. I feel like we're waving a shiny prize in the demon king's face, saying come on and get it! Sure, this camp will protect you, but will the gods?"

Fenryn paused. "No." Her answer was no more than a breath. "They will not aid me. Maybe Loki will, but that is self-serving. When everything –" She closed her eyes and took a steadying breath. "Olympus helped me before, though, to call on them again…it would be an abuse of their kindness."

The two walked towards the Valkyries. A woman clad in golden armor, long red hair tied away from her freckled face, blocked Marron's way with her golden staff. "Fenryn only. You may wait here." Her voice stern with authority, wings tucked in tight behind her back.

Fenryn chuckled and placed a gentle hand on Valkyrie's cheek. "Oh Calliope, how I missed you. Marron is my guard for the day. If I leave him behind, he will start howling at the gates."

Calliope's brown eyes narrowed. "Just this once." She withdrew her staff but held her position guarding the Valkyrie camp.

Fenryn smirked. "Where can I find Brynhildr? I

need to buy new armor."

"She is in the shop by the agility track, but Fen…we kept your old leathers. If you want them, no one has touched them. We knew you'd return. We are prepared for the coming storm."

"Let's hope I can prevent the storm altogether." Fenryn placed a hand on Calliope's shoulder. "Where can I find them?"

"The shifter must wait outside the tent, but Brynhildr has all of your items." Calliope gestured towards the grand, golden tent at the center of the camp.

"Thank you, Cal."

"You would have been an amazing Valkyrie, Fen. We have missed you every day since…" Calliope closed her mouth remembering the day Loki declared Fenryn's betrothal, ending her time with the Valkyries.

Fenryn bit back her tears and nodded, making her way to the encroaching tent.

"A Valkyrie?" Marron looked at the female beside him, taking in the formal cadence her walk had adopted since greeting Calliope. Shoulders back, chin up, assertive. "I didn't think you could leave once you were enlisted."

"You aren't supposed to be able to." Fenryn's voice broke and both hands grasped her wrists, hiding the burns.

They reached the tent at last. Marron could hear Fenryn's heart racing. He stepped in front of her. "I don't know what you will face there, but you will overcome it. Everyone who needs to pay, will." His sapphire eyes burned with ferocity.

Fenryn took another steadying breath and squared her shoulders. "Thank you."

"I'll be right here when you're done."

She looked at the man, at his sure stance, the tattoos peeking from under his sleeves, his red hair practically glowing in the setting sun. She shouldn't trust him. His presence should not reassure her. And yet…

Shaking her head, she entered the enclosure.

"Finally," Brynhildr exclaimed, her white hair braided into a crown atop her head, wings relaxed with the joy at seeing Fenryn, rushed from the wall of swords and armor taking up the majority of the tent towards her once favorite recruit. "My Fenryn has returned!" She took Fenryn's face between her hands, stroking her cheeks tenderly. "Gods, I cannot believe you went to your asshole father before you came here." Fenryn was suddenly wrapped in an embrace she had long forgotten. "Look at you! I searched everywhere for you these past two centuries. I prayed for any sign that you were okay. I am so glad you were found."

Fenryn let out a breath before embracing the giant muscular woman. "You have not changed, Brynhildr."

"And why would I? I am perfection." Brynhildr winked and stepped away from her friend. "I suppose you're here for your leathers."

"That would be correct." Fenryn looked around the tent, wishing she could locate them out in the open.

"You know, I can't just give them back to you. You must prove you're still worthy. It would dishonor my young recruits if I were simply to hand over leathers like that."

Fenryn's heart raced. She raised her chin and looked the leader in her eyes as she nodded. "I accept your challenge." A proud smile snuck its way across Fenryn's face.

Brynhildr's eyes sparked with excitement. "*Wonderful.* Follow me." She threw an arm over Fenryn's shoulders and led her to the sparring ring.

Fenryn made eye contact with Marron, sending the only warning she could before they entered to the sword fighting ring. Young Valkyrie recruits circled the fence cheering for Fenryn.

"Valkyries!" Brynhildr shouted. "Come join us! Fenryn will be fighting for the honor to regain her leathers today. Now, typically, I would let you fight someone who I know is up to your speed. However, when you were so rudely ripped away from us all those years ago, Fenryn, you were my equal. Defeat me, and you may have your leathers back."

A collective gasp rippled through the camp. To defeat Brynhildr was unheard of. Fenryn had only done so twice in the past.

Marron rushed towards Fenryn. He wanted to warn her how dangerous this endeavor could be. Calliope stopped him.

"If you want even one more discussion with Fenryn, you will respect her honor and allow her to participate in this fight. She would not take kindly from being pulled from a Brynhildr's challenge. This trial is about far more than sword play, prince. It is restoration of pride and hope."

He watched Fenryn as she strapped a breastplate to her chest. Her face lit with determination and perhaps by pure joy.

The Valkyrie and Shifter met again in the ring, each of them grinning mischievously at the other.

"Begin," Calliope ordered.

To Marron, Calliope explained, "Three hits or one fatal blow, determines the winner. Blood will be drawn, so brace yourself. I don't care if you *are* her mate. If you rush in there, one of them will kill you. Valkyries are just as lethal as the berserkers, and reckless in the heat of battle."

Marron swallowed. Was he that obvious? Fenryn and Brynhildr danced around one another warily.

Calliope sighed. "No, fool, you are not. I can

hear everyone's thoughts. It's a damned nuisance. Moreover, your auras are trying to connect. Anyone who can see your aura will know. Your behavior is telling, though. If you want to hide it, you better fix your face." She gestured to his entire countenance.

Marron grunted and returned his attention to Fenryn. It was she who received the first strike from Brynhildr's blade. Fenryn bared her teeth right before Brynhildr threw her to the side. Fenryn blocked the following downward blow, swiping her feet under the Valkyrie. Brynhildr fell to the ground, earning the hilt of Fenryn's sword to her temple. Blood trickled down the Valkyrie's brow.

"That's one." Calliope leaned on the barricade. Marron was inclined to follow suit.

The women rose to their feet. Brynhildr struck first, lethal, and sure. Yet somehow Fenryn predicted the movement. She sidestepped and spun around the Valkyrie, landing another strike on Brynhildr's back. The Valkyrie spat blood into the dirt and ran at Fenryn. Fenryn dropped to her knees and raised her blade above her head. Brynhildr crashed hard, metal clashing and ringing across the field. Fenryn loosened her grip on the fire within her, allowing the burning power to come forward onto the blade. The Valkyrie was so overcome with surprise, that Fenryn was able to get to her feet and thrust the blade just a hair's breadth away from her neck.

Brynhildr laughed outright. "Oh, I miss your spirit, Fenryn. Your leathers are yours once again. Bring the Valkyries honor when you wear them."

Fenryn wiped the sweat from her brow. "Thank you for the opportunity to earn them back." Beaming with pride, she clasped Brynhildr's forearm in a formal handshake.

Calliope glanced toward the prince. "Now you may go tell our girl how stupid you thought her decision was." She clapped Marron on his shoulder and turned back to her post.

Fenryn sauntered over to Marron, unsheathed her sword, and pointed it towards the prince. "I do not know you, *prince*. I do not understand or like the fact that I shifted in your presence. You have yet to earn my full trust, and I will do anything to protect my people. I don't care what you think your connection to me is. The fact that Meraena trusts you in her home and allows you to fade in and out is the only reason I continue to trust you. Do you understand?"

Marron's deep blue eyes gleamed with the challenge. "Oh, princess, our *connection* is beyond either of our control. But I understand. If you need to fight me, Fenryn, we can enter the ring at any time."

He gave her a wink and pushed the blade aside with his forefinger. She snarled as she ripped off her breastplate and revealed the sweat-soaked shirt beneath, unknowingly giving Marron a beautiful view. He cleared his throat. A more pressing thought crossed his mind. Who *were* her people? Who did she save from Apopis? He didn't dare ask those questions yet.

"You fight well, Ryn. You clearly remember how to fight like a Valkyrie."

The pride on Fenryn's face quickly changed into a blush as she glanced down at her breasts, which were nearly on full display. "I'm going to change."

Marron watched her strut to the tent and fought the urge to follow and rip Evan's damn shirt off her body.

He huffed a breath and looked up at the fading daylight. What was he going to do? His fiancé was at his father's castle, probably sobbing about his absence. He covered his face and groaned into his hands.

"I'm starving. Can we find something to eat and head home?" Fenryn declared as she returned, peering around the camp for anything that resembled a mess hall.

He was looking at what he wanted. Gods, this woman in emerald and gold Valkyrie leathers that hugged every curve of her body captivated his mind. Her sword strapped to her back and sheathed dagger strapped to her left thigh, she was a lethal vision. His mouth went dry.

She huffed a laugh and patted Marron's cheek. "There, there, Prince. Words will come. Give it time. I, however, am not waiting to eat. I think I heard that the berserkers are grilling tonight." She rested a hand on the bejeweled hilt of her dagger and proceeded to the other side of the camp.

Marron caught Calliope watching the exchange.

She shook her head, chuckling at the gaping fool he was. Rolling his eyes, he followed Fenryn, until suddenly he wished he had not.

All eyes in camp were transfixed on the beauty in front of them. Fenryn captivating more people than just the prince. A low growl escaped Marron's throat as he found Evan.

"You have definitely seen better days, my friend," Evan laughed, throwing an arm across Marron's shoulder. "They are a bunch of horny pups. Ignore them."

Fenryn approached the cooks and grabbed a plate. Maybe the leathers were a mistake, she thought. Everyone was watching her. Still, they were all she had.

You are my *daughter. You will not be ashamed.* Loki's mantra from her childhood rang through her head.

Looking back, perhaps being Loki's daughter wasn't a great reason not to feel shame. He had certainly caused plenty of chaos that would bring shame to others. But she was Fenryn. She had survived Apopis and saved her people. For that, she would stand tall.

A young berserker recruit filled her plate. His gaze drifted down, lower than her eyes.

"Pup, I will warn you once. Give women the respect of looking them in the eye and holding a civilized conversation before you start undressing them with your eyes," Fenryn fumed, lifting her dagger from its sheath. She pointed the tip to the boy's trembling Adam's apple as she snatched her plate from him. A fierce blush swept across his face.

Evan came up to her and smiled. "Flynn is a flirt even to the fire sprites. It will cost him one day. Come on, I've got us a seat with Marron in the back."

Thank Odin, Fenryn thought. She didn't think she could manage to eat in front of the dining hall. Ignoring everyone's stare, Fenryn followed the general and sat beside Marron in the back.

"I heard you put on quite a show for the Valkyries," Evan said around a mouthful of roasted pork.

Fenryn blushed and tucked a stray piece of hair behind her ear. "I used to be one of them, before my father accepted the marriage proposal. This was my home after my training with Tyr." Fenryn closed her eyes, trying to block the memory from that day.

Fenryn struck the target dead center. Calliope shouted praise from the stands. They had gone through a terrible battle just days ago. Everyone was enjoying their time drinking and shooting targets instead of people in the barracks. Several Valkyries slipped out to the neighboring training ring for young berserkers the previous night. While most Valkyries were celibate, some saw that as a rule that was meant to be broken after battle.

Calliope handed Fenryn a stein of mead and began singing along with the Valkyries gathered around the fire.

Fenryn smiled and gazed towards Brynhildr. Despite their victory, their ruthless leader had a pained look on her face.

"Bryn!" Fenryn swayed and laughed as she rushed towards her best friend. The blonde beauty met Fenryn's gaze with tear-filled eyes. "What? What is it?" She reached for her sword, ready to slay anyone responsible for that look on Bryn's face.

"Fenryn, I need you to stay calm. We will find a way out of this. We will fight." Bryn grasped Fenryn's shoulders tightly. *"You have been sold to marriage. You are to be wed to Apopis, the Demon King."*

Fenryn's breath escaped her lungs. Her knees felt like they might give out. "No, Loki would never. I'm a Valkyrie! I earned my title! I belong here! I have said my vows."

"It is done." Bryn's voice broke. "But I will do what I can to protect you from this atrocity. Follow me."

The two women held hands as they entered Bryn's tent, where a shaman awaited them.

"I don't understand." Fenryn backed up.

"The Demon King is desperate for heirs or demons. He will take what he can. Layla will tattoo a sigil on your scalp, where Apopis can never see it. It will prevent a pregnancy from ever taking root."

Fenryn shook with – rage? Fear? Both? Nodding, she sat before Layla, the shaman. Hours of tattooing passed by before the shaman finally declared her work was done.

"Take this with you." Layla pressed an opal into Fenryn's palm. "Should Apopis ever discover your tattoo, make sure to break this. I will come and carve the sigil into your bones. Let us pray it doesn't come to that."

Fenryn felt a tear escape her eye and slide down her cheek. She put the opal in the pocket inside her breastplate and nodded. "Thank you."

Marron's hand found Fenryn's knee, interrupting her recollection. She met his stare and gave him a subtle nod of thanks before slowly moving her leg away. She wasn't willing to acknowledge the spark that their touch ignited.

She took a bite off her plate; it could have been her favorite meal in the world and still the taste would have escaped her. Why hadn't she fought harder?

But how can you fight a god like Loki?

Evan handed Fenryn a stein. "Drink up, princess. We will vanquish the gods tomorrow."

Fenryn laughed, rolling her eyes. "I am no princess. I think tomorrow I'd like to work on shifting and finding my wolf form. We will need it for what is to come."

Evan pointed his mug towards Marron. "That's his territory. I only shift into my berserker form. Marron can shift into anything he wishes."

Marron now wore a mischievous grin. "Think you can keep up, princess?"

"I'm going to set you both on fire if you keep calling me princess," Fenryn grumbled and finished the last of her mead, enjoying the sweet honey flavor dancing on the tip of her tongue.

"Ah, but you would have to find me first." Marron winked and vanished immediately.

Fenryn gasped and looked at Evan, who shook his head and rolled his eyes.

"That dumbass is such a show-off."

Marron's laugh still sounded next to Fenryn. She reached out, a hand landing on his chest. The male reappeared, full of pride, eyebrow raised. "If you wanted to feel me up, princess, all you had to do was ask."

Fenryn scoffed and smacked the prince on the back of his head. "Fool."

Marron grinned. "Practice with me, Ryn, and I'll teach you to hide in the folds of the realms when fading."

She smiled and shook her head as she threw her plate in the trash.

The men followed suit. Evan informed his captain that he would be on leave for the next few days. Marron stood near Fenryn as they waited.

"Tell me more about Hecate, please," Marron implored as they waited for Evan.

"Hecate was a sister I never had. We met when I was very young, maybe fifty years or so. She was there for everything, my initiation with the Valkyries, my marriage, all of it. Beyond a shadow of a doubt, I always knew I could trust her. If I knew it wouldn't put my citizens in danger, I would go to her now." Fenryn watched Evan make his way back.

"I understand. Evan and I have been that for one another. We met here on the training fields."

She couldn't help noticing the tug in her chest and the radiating warmth she felt from Marron's presence beside her. She frowned at the prince.

"What?" his brow furrowed in genuine confusion.

"No." She glared at him.

Marron sighed in understanding. "This is not the time or the place."

"There will *be* no time or place, prince. Never again will I be–"

Marron was about to interrupt as Evan returned, shooting them both a quizzical look.

Fenryn fumed and crossed her arms around her chest. Marron huffed and faded himself out of the barracks.

"He is going to raise unwanted attention." Evan shook his head and extended his hand to Fenryn. "Let's go."

She absently nodded and took his hand, cursing the fates and their cruel games.

Evan dropped Fenryn off in Meraena's apartment before leaving to visit Meraena. Fenryn couldn't stop seething. How dare the fates! Hadn't she been through enough? Wasn't sacrificing two hundred years in a shifted form enough? Why Marron? She knew nothing about him, but he was a male. She had already been shackled to one by force. Did the fates now want to do the same thing her father once had done?

She screamed into the emptiness of the apartment around her, unintentionally catching fire as sobs escaped her broken mind and body. Fenryn took herself to the shower and ran cold water over her flames.

CHAPTER 9

Fenryn lost track of how much time she spent in the water. She must have eventually fallen asleep.

Dreams of iron shackles, stone floors and demon predators surrounding her consumed her mind.

"You think a minor spell can keep you from me? I will find you. You are mine. *Remember what I did to you when you ran, before? That will be* nothing *compared to what is to come."*

A scream of terror tore through Fenryn. Suddenly, Marron appeared in the bathroom A towel soon covered her shivering body as he lifted her out of the freezing water. She swung at him, legs kicking, and managed to connect a fist to his jaw.

"You're safe. I have you. You're safe." Ignoring the blood trailing from his lip, Marron carried Fenryn to the guest bedroom and laid her on the bed. He covered the violently shaking woman tightly in the duvet.

"He found me." Fenryn clung to herself. The words came out in anguished rasps. "He won't stop. He won't. He found me. He was in my mind!"

Marron's jaw ticked as he stood at the edge of the bed, securing the blanket around Fenryn. "I'm going to hold you, princess. I warn you; I'm not giving you any other option. Your lips are blue."

Marron slowly eased his way down and curled around her trembling body. "I have you. You're safe. I will never let that *filth* lay hands on you again. You're safe."

"No one is safe." She turned in to his chest, clinging tight. "Especially now. You will all die. It will all be my fault. It will all be my fault again. I can't..."

Marron smoothed Fenryn's damp hair and held her close to him. "This is not your fault. The Demon King is the one responsible for this. He *will* pay for what he has taken from you."

Fenryn's shaking finally subsided, her body giving way to exhaustion. "You cannot be my mate. You will die. He will kill you."

"It would be an honor to be your mate, Fenryn. Sleep now, princess." Marron placed a tender kiss on her forehead as her consciousness gave way to the night.

Marron considered sleep for a moment, but instead took stock of the scars marring Fenryn's back. He counted each one, committing them to memory and imagining every conceivable way he would repay Apopis the favor. Marron found thirty-one scars on her upper back alone.

Hours passed by and Fenryn slept soundly on Marron's chest. He knew he should return home and send his fiancé away. But Fenryn's deep, calm breaths held him firmly in place.

It was the fear and hypothermia he had felt through the mate bond, despite it being incomplete. That had been enough to set him into action that evening.

Just as Kornelia, his unwanted fiancé, knocked on his bedroom door, Marron felt his chest contract with a fear that was not his. By the time he said he was unable to dine with her that evening, his teeth had begun to chatter. Gods, going home was going to be a nightmare.

A soft snore left Fenryn's open mouth. Marron chuckled and caressed her cheek. He eased down into the bed and closed his eyes. "I will protect you," he murmured into her hair before he, too, fell asleep.

Fenryn woke to the warmth and steady breathing of a sleeping man beside her. She slipped off the bed clutching a blanket to her chest and rummaged through the drawers for something that might fit her. *Damn it, I need to find a store*, she thought.

"You don't have to cover up on my account." Marron's voice was a sleepy rasp that did things to Fenryn's core she would rather ignore.

"Neither time that you've seen me naked has been by my invitation." Fenryn huffed at Meraena's drawers, which were empty save for one of Meraena's tiny sundresses. Fenryn was afraid to even consider that. "Though, I do thank you for… last night."

She held up Meraena's dress and frowned at the hemline, which reached just two inches below her ass.

Marron propped himself on his elbow, grinning with pure male desire. "If you wear that, we won't be leaving the apartment."

She groaned. "Meraena is impossibly small."

"Her mother is not a giant." Marron chuckled before vanishing and reappearing with a dress shirt.

"Today, you wear mine," he growled, possession ringing clear in his voice.

"We are not mated, Marron. You do not own me." She took the shirt grudgingly and glared at the impossible man.

"No one will *ever* own you, Fenryn." His voice was steel as his gaze bore into her. Heat flooded between Fenryn's legs. "I would only wish to be your partner."

"Then you would be sentencing yourself to death." She dropped the blanket and held his stare before turning and retrieving her underwear from the bathroom floor.

Marron watched every sway of her hips. His pants became entirely too tight.

Fenryn returned wearing her black leather pants and Marron's violet satin shirt, which she had taken the liberty of tying around her waist, exposing small slivers of her midsection.

"Gods, help me," Marron groaned under his breath. "Let's get you to a store, before I regret all my actions for the foreseeable future."

Fenryn blushed and pulled her hair into a high ponytail. "Coffee first. Then, shopping. Then, you teach me how to fade. I used to do it all the time, but I just don't remember everything yet. It keeps coming to me in flashes."

Marron took a deep breath and nodded. "Somewhere in there, I need to have a meeting with my father. Ending my betrothal will not be easy."

Fenryn stopped at the door, turning to look at Marron. "We could petition the fates to end our bond. It's been done before." Granted the last couple who received their request, died during the severing of the bond, but maybe their case would be different. The severance had only been done once in history in which the couple lived.

Marron's face went blank. A schooled expression of a politician. He wanted to ask if she remembered the story of those who ended their fated match and how their minds withered. "Is that what you want?"

"Wouldn't it be for the best?" Fenryn fidgeted with the hair tie at the end of her braid.

"I think a future with you is a worthy adventure." Marron stood up from the bed and walked towards Fenryn.

"You are a fool." Fenryn rolled her eyes and left the apartment, padding down the cool hallway. Notes of lavender filled the air.

Marron followed on her heel as they left the building, and whispered coyly into her ear, "Better a fool than a pessimist."

Growling at the goosebumps that now covered her body, Fenryn glared at the prince. "It's not pessimism if I know it to be true."

Marron smirked and walked proudly beside her, not paying mind to anyone behind him on the brick lined sidewalk. "You have never seen me in battle. You barely know what I am capable of. Maybe taking down Apopis will be a piece of cake with me as your equal."

"You don't know what you say. Marron –"

"Mmm, say my name again. It sounds good on your lips." Marron growled as he skipped in front of Fenryn, walking smoothly backwards as she shoved past him.

"Quit flirting with me and listen!" Fenryn's hands flew to her hips as she stomped her foot on the pavement.

Marron grinned with a wink. "But you are so much fun when you're all hot and bothered."

Heat rushed to Fenryn's cheeks. "I am not hot and bothered. I am annoyed." She focused on the streetlight, waiting for it to allow them to cross the street.

"That is not what your scent told me in the apartment, princess."

Fenryn placed her hands on Marron's shoulders abruptly, eyes searing with flames and anger. "Listen. To. Me."

Marron was unprepared for the vision that suddenly filled his mind. A gasp escaped him as he witnessed such horror that no one should ever have been subjected to.

Fenryn laid on the stone floor, still tied to the ground with the iron shackles. Apopis stood bare above her, his onyx skin, muscular form nearly blending into the pitch darkness of the cellar. Only the red glow of his eyes made him visible.

"You have refused the marriage bed long enough. You have brought this on yourself, Fenryn. I have been more than patient with you. I will have an heir to my throne. The fates told me of your destiny. Your child will change the course of the fae. I will see it done!"

He summoned a blade from Gods knew where and sliced down Fenryn's body, shredding her clothes and her skin along with it.

Fenryn bit back her cries of pain. She would not give him the satisfaction. She closed her eyes and turned her head as her tears fell to the biting stone.

Apopis grabbed her by her hair, scalp screaming with the strength of his pull. "You will watch."

Fenryn spat in the bastard's face.

A dark chuckle left the monster's throat as he wiped the spit from his cheek. Then he tore the blade across hers. Blood seeped out as Apopis dropped himself onto her body, releasing a black mist around them.

"You are mine!" *Apopis declared as his body consumed hers.*

Marron jumped back and screamed every curse he knew in every language. Fenryn shook from the memory. The fucking memories that kept flooding her.

"Fenryn." He approached her slowly.

She pulled a dagger from the fold of her shirt and held it to his throat. "Don't. I did not choose to share that memory. I *never* would have shared that memory. Do. Not."

Marron shut his mouth and ran his hand through his long red hair. "Coffee."

She put the dagger back and nodded. "*All* the coffee."

CHAPTER 10

They walked in silence to a skyscraper mall, windows glowing in the midmorning sunlight. Marron joined her for coffee, which they ordered at a shop just inside the mall and drank in silence.

"Do you mind if I let you shop on your own, and I will meet you back here at the coffee shop when you're done? I have to talk to Midas before things get out of hand."

"How will you know when I am done?" Fenryn looked around the mall, feeling rather small and a bit lost.

Marron's voice entered her mind.

Like this, princess.

"How?" Her eyes went wide.

You opened the bridge between us when you shared the vision. I could feel you in my mind after the vision ended. All mates share a mind link.

Can you hear everything?

Only if I try to. Marron winked at her.

Don't try. She glared at his beaming face. *I'll let you know when I am finished.*

"Do you have money?" Marron asked, suddenly feeling foolish for not asking sooner.

Fenryn laughed. "Yes, prince. I have money. I grabbed what I had from the Valkyrie camp yesterday."

Marron nodded. "Reach out if you need anything."

Fenryn nodded. "Goodbye, Marron."

He grinned at her before vanishing away.

Fenryn huffed and finished the last sip of her coffee. One step at a time. She just had to start with clothes, then move on to the next step. She could do this. Fenryn walked down the expanse of the mall, glancing at the many shop windows. Everything was floral and pastel for spring. After an hour of walking through shop after shop, Fenryn was about ready to set the entire place on fire.

That's considered arson, my dear, and rather frowned upon in Olympian malls. Marron chuckled through their connection.

Where the Hel are the not *pink clothes?* Fenryn

glared at a mannequin in an all-pink tulle dress.

It's not her fault! Marron laughed. *Try Seph's on the second floor. They may be more your style.*

Trusting his advice, Fenryn went to the second floor and found Seph's. She sent an entire string of foul words down the bond when she glanced at the window display.

Fool, I do not need lingerie.

He laughed. *Go in. There are clothes in the back. Sex is not* all *I think about, princess.*

She growled at him and went in despite herself. He was right, though. In the back, she found dresses, blouses, and everything she could need. The store truly won her over when the options were all in colors that didn't resemble the Norse goddess of spring, Iduna's, throw up.

"May I help you?" A blonde pixie glided up to Fenryn, her black tulle dress swaying in the movement.

"Uh, yes. I don't have any idea what size I should wear, but I need new everything. I prefer greens, gold, black, red, or deep purple. Leather is always a plus, but I need dresses too."

The pixie beamed with excitement. "Follow me and we will get your measurements."

Fenryn lost track of time. She left the store excited to have a wardrobe of her own.

Mm, you look absolutely divine, Ryn.

Fenryn blushed, smoothing the blood-red tulle skirt extending below the black leather corset which now held her dagger by her side. Sheer red tights hugged her legs. Black combat boots completed her ensemble.

How's your father? Did he accept that the fates have selected your mate for you?

Marron groaned. *He is currently breaking everything in his study. I give him about twenty more minutes of tantrum before he comes back with a royal decree.*

Fenryn laughed and adjusted the numerous bags in her arms.

You should really practice fading. It would lighten the load immensely.

Alas, prince, my teacher seems to be held up. I am going to have to hoof it for now.

"Unacceptable." Marron appeared in front of her, taking her breath away. "Take my hand, princess."

She shook her head and rolled her eyes at the man's audacity. "You are reckless for a man who prefers his fading to remain a secret."

He placed a finger on her lips and wagged his eyebrows. "Shh."

They were immediately transported to Meraena's apartment. The prince faded out as quickly as he appeared.

"Fool," she chuckled and began putting her clothes away.

Ahh, but a charming fool, nonetheless.

Get out of my head, fool. She laughed.

Block me, then.

Fenryn frowned. Could she? She pictured a barrier of black abyss and focused on that void taking over all of her mind.

Very misty, my dear. Try something more… sturdy. Think brick or granite.

She went with obsidian. She left it in place for 20 minutes, before her mind became weary.

Effective, princess.

I am a demigod, not a princess.

Is that what I shall call you?

She groaned. *No. Please.*

Very well. Oh, the royal decree is a ball in honor of our mate bond.

Fenryn froze in the middle of putting her clothes away, a thong still in hand.

Wear that. Just that, to the ball. He sent her an image of him winking.

I can't just come out! Apopis will be there! It will be a direct threat.

Let him. I'd love a chance to express my thoughts about your previous marriage. Venom and rage dripped off every one of Marron's words.

He could kill everyone in the castle with just one thought, Marron! Call off the ball. We are not ready. I am not ready.

There is no calling off King Midas. I will get with Evan and Meraena. We will also meet with your father, right? We have allies everywhere. We can do this, Ryn.

What about your fiancé?

Marron huffed down the link. *She will be an emotional mess, but she will survive.*

Fenryn put the last of her clothes in the dresser. *Are we going to practice fading or not?*

Meet me at the berserker barracks.

How? That's not helpful. It's just an order! She crossed her arms and glared at her reflection sitting atop the dresser mirror.

Imagine it. Want it. Think of the smell, the feel, the sound. Picture everything.

Fenryn took a deep breath and closed her eyes, envisioning the field where the sprites offered her the sunburst day lily. She inhaled the fresh scent of the flower and moss surrounding her.

The overwhelming sound of clanging swords and roaring berserkers consumed Fenryn's focus. She opened her eyes to see Marron smiling, arms crossed, and chest puffed with pride.

"Well done, princess. Now go back home and change for battle. We are sparring today. I'll wait here," He winked at her, making a show of sitting in the grass.

She stuck her tongue out at the insufferably handsome man dressed in slate gray and gold Olympian leathers, arm tattoos on full display, bending with every flex and movement of his arms.

Marron's grin deepened. His voice dropped lower as he said, "Or I could come along with you. We could do something about those thoughts running rampant in your mind."

She threw up her mental wall and attempted to return to Meraena's apartment. It took a long ten minutes before her body returned to her room, her hair disheveled and her balance off. Her reflection in the mirror looked like she went through a wind tunnel.

She immediately went to the closet and changed into the new ensemble she bought that morning. Emerald boning wrapped around her chest, as the leather conformed to the curves of her body. She threw her hair into a high ponytail and strapped her sword to a sheath across her back.

Focusing on the sparring field, Fenryn faded beside Marron. This time it was smoother, but her heart still raced with nerves from the endeavor.

"Let's go, prince."

Marron's gaze darkened as he took her in. "By all means, Ryn. Show me what you're made of."

Fenryn walked to the center of the ring and drew her sword.

Marron faded directly behind her; dagger pressed to the small of her back. "First thing, princess: don't fight fair. Fight to win." His lips grazed her ear as he withdrew.

She ignored the goosebumps his touch evoked and swiped a leg behind her, knocking the arrogant turd to the ground.

"Good, Ryn." He smirked as he jumped to his feet and withdrew his sword.

She allowed her building rage and contempt to well in her chest as she charged. To hell with sparring ring etiquette. To hell with formalities. Marron's eyes lit with the challenge as he met her blow and knocked her sword across the ring. Fenryn withdrew the dagger from her boot and dove for the prince's ankles. He danced to the side, missing the strike by an inch. She turned and went for his throat. He blocked her movement and struck the dagger out of her hand.

She roared and charged, tackling the man at the waist. He controlled the movement, rolling on top of her pinning her arms to the ground. "Are you finished?"

She panted as sweat dripped down her brow. "Never."

"Good. Now get up and show me real strategy." He offered her a calloused hand up.

They fought relentlessly, fading and reappearing, catching one another off guard, until ultimately, they fell into rhythm and began anticipating each other's movements. Steel clashed with steel. Fenryn's arms burned with each impact and damn if it didn't bring back the joy of being a Valkyrie. She reveled in the feeling. Lethal fire rose to her eyes as she surged forward. Marron bared his teeth in a menacing grin, happy to meet her stride for stride. The light of day waned as Marron dropped himself to the dirt on the ring's ground, panting.

"I'd say that was a successful training session." He closed his eyes, catching his breath.

Fenryn considered him for a moment, then

dropped to the dust next to him. "When is the ball?"

He turned his head and took in her sweaty and dirt-covered face. He wiped away some of the filth with a laugh, only to smudge it across her cheek. He grimaced. "Next Friday."

"We will need every soldier stationed and ready for battle." Her breathing was still ragged from sparring as she stared up into the twilight sky. "I will stay here tonight and visit my father."

Marron opened his mouth to argue, but he was interrupted by a looming shadow.

"No need to visit me, Fenryn. What is it you need? The sprites are such gossips," Loki smirked as he inspected the dirt beneath his fingernails. "I do assume this has something to do with the growing bond between you two. The violet link is rather remarkable for mates. Usually, links are a thin line connecting the pair. Yours is thick and bold, almost consuming both of you at once. It is unlike anything I have seen. Oh, and prince? I do hope you are aware she is not accessing the full extent of her powers. This is just a drop. More of a tease, really. Do try to coax more out of my stubborn child.

She will need it. My armies will be waiting for your word, my love."

Loki vanished with a wink, leaving Marron and Fenryn still laying in dirt speechless.

"I hate him." Fenryn ground out as she stood and brushed off the dust from her clothes.

"Do you?" Marron hedged. He felt like he needed true confirmation of Fenryn's feelings before he could share his own.

A frustrated growl escaped her throat as she rubbed her face. "Yes. No… Sometimes. I hate what he put me through just for his games. But there are some lessons he taught me that are invaluable. I don't know. He's more of an annoying brother than a caring father."

Marron could see that.

"I don't trust him. He will supply me with aid, but until when? When does my situation stop lending itself to his entertainment? Loki is loyal only to himself."

"Let's head back to Scynthia. I think we have earned a trip to Margot's."

"What I have earned is a shower. Then, *maybe*, I will go to whatever Margot's is." Fenryn winked at the prince, gave a mock salute, and left for the apartment.

Once she arrived, she peeled the drenched leather from her skin with a groan. She relished the ache of muscles she hadn't used in centuries. Gods, it felt good to be back in her fae form again. Loki was right, though. She used to be unstoppable. Armies would cower before the sight of her wolf form sheathed in flame.

Turning the hot water on, her reflection in the mirror caught her eye. Apopis had destroyed her body. Burns and gouges marred nearly every surface of her skin. The memory of iron being shoved in the cuts to prevent her from healing sent a chill up her spine. The injection they had given her to prevent her flames, shifting and fading – he would pay. They would all pay.

CHAPTER 11

Fenryn showered for longer than she intended, but once she got out, she felt renewed and energized for anything the night may bring.

Anything, princess?

Get out of my head, fool.

His deep laugh spread warmth between her thighs. *Ahh, but where is the fun in that?*

Since you are here, what should I wear to Margot's?

I don't know. Do you dance?

She stood in front of her closet wrapped in a towel. Water dripped down her legs. She grimaced at her clothes. *Does a waltz count?*

Marron chuckled. *Not at Margot's. Wear something light. It will be hot, and you will sweat.*

She pursed her lips as she planted her hands on her hips. Dancing. Modern dancing at that. She eventually landed on a black lace tank top with a red satin underlay finished with black leather shorts, long enough to conceal a dagger, but short enough to allow for plenty of movement. Black combat boots completed the outfit. She applied a layer of matte lipstick to her lips, the shade resemblant to a luscious merlot. Satisfied, she braided the sides of her hair and pulled it back into a high ponytail.

Ready.

"Good." Marron faded in front of her and blinked at the fae woman, mouth bobbing like a fish.

She patted his cheek, offering him a small smirk. "Let's go."

"I've changed my mind." Marron stared at Fenryn's ass as she sauntered towards the door.

"Too late for that, prince. I'm all dressed and ready to see how dancing has changed since I was young." She peered over her shoulder and winked at the male as she unlocked the door and stepped into the hallway.

"Gods spare me." Marron muttered, rubbing his face as he followed behind. He prayed he wouldn't have to kill anyone who dared touch his woman tonight.

As they walked the dark streets, Marron explained how to work the new iPhone, showing

Fenryn how to set up passcodes and lock screens. He had already taken the liberty of adding his grinning selfie to the home screen. Fenryn caught on fairly quick, having watched others over the years.

The pair walked seven blocks to meet up with Meraena and Evan at the front doors of a two-story tan brick building, loud up-tempo music seeping out the doorway and metal framed windows. Balconies held couples looking for fresh air. A large pink neon sign read Margot's above the elegant black doors.

Meraena let out a low whistle. "I see the wolf is out to play. Let's get it!" She entwined her arm in Fenryn's and pushed through the wooden doorway.

Evan chuckled and shoved Marron. "You're so fucked."

"Shut up." Marron barged through the doors and went straight for the bar, where he ordered a neat whiskey.

Evan grabbed an IPA and leaned back on his elbows to watch his mate dance freely on the floor. Fenryn observed Meraena's loose and rhythmic style and compared it to those around her. Everything was unstructured and very much geared towards lust and sex. The entire bar stunk of arousal. Minotaur's, humans, sprites, even some berserkers from Asgard gathered on the floor, loosing themselves to the music.

"I'm going to need a drink before I can dance like that." Fenryn laughed and excused herself to the bar.

"What can I get you, darlin'?" a male siren mused as he leaned towards Fenryn, taking a deep breath, inhaling her scent.

"About five feet of space, thank you." Fenryn fought the song that attempted to fill her head, slamming up the mental wall like she had practiced earlier with Marron. The siren scoffed and turned his back to her, looking for its next prey.

"Amaretto sour," she called to the bartender.

"Some things never change," a dark voice she knew too well whispered in her ear.

Darkness shrouded Fenryn. Her heart hammered in her chest and a cold sweat covered her body.

"Leave. These are innocent people." Fenryn's

voice was barely a whisper. It was all she could manage as she reached for her dagger.

"No one is truly innocent, are they, Fenryn?" A frozen claw slid down her cheek and left a trail of blood in its wake.

"Come home, Fen." Apopis crooned. "We have so much we left unfinished." His shadow claws raked down her shoulders and trailed across her midsection. "Bring that fated mate of yours. We can end your tie before it becomes a bind." A single talon dug into her wrist. Fenryn bit down on her cry of pain just as the darkness around her vanished along with Apopis. Suddenly, she was staring at a furious and terrified Marron. Her drink dripped down her hand as the glass had shattered in her terrified grip.

Evan raised his hand to the bartender. "Another round for my friend, please."

The bartender nodded. Fenryn shook the glass and the blood from her hand. She stared blankly at the wooden bar now soaked in her mess. "I'm gonna… Bathroom."

Marron looked like he was about to voice an objection, but Meraena stepped up and placed an arm on the small of Fenryn's back.

"Let's get you cleaned up." Her friend directed them to the restroom and went to work washing away the blood.

"He's getting stronger." Fenryn's body shook. "He may not have been able to fully fade to me now, but it's only a matter of time before he can."

"Then we ward the hell out of your body and mind, Fenryn. And you keep training. You never stop until that son of a bitch is dead, burned and buried with iron coating his bones. We don't rest until this is done. Tonight, we saw what he is capable of doing right now. It was merely a jump-scare and a few parlor tricks. We can all make someone bleed. So, we drink. We dance. We allow ourselves to be *free.* You do not bend to filth like him. You are *Fenryn,* for gods' sake. You will slay that motherfucker."

Fenryn studied her lavender-haired friend for a moment before laughing ceaselessly. "How much have you had to drink?"

Meraena waved her hand. "My dad was difficult this weekend, but such is the way of being a god's daughter, as you very well know. Are you ready to get back out there?"

Fenryn looked at herself in the mirror. Her skin was already mending and healing itself. "I'm ready."

Evan and Marron were waiting for them near the bathroom. Marron extended an amaretto sour to Fenryn.

"Thank you." She smiled and took a sip, savoring the sour's bite. "It's perfect."

"As are you." Marron extended a hand. "Dance with me."

His eyes met hers and her heart leapt into action. Marron's words were a request, not a command. He was leaving the choice entirely up to her. She drained her cup, set it on a nearby table without care and followed him to the dance floor.

The music's rhythm was now slow and steady. Marron held one of Fenryn's hands up in his and pressed the other to the small of her back, moving their hips closer to each other. They swayed together, Fenryn laying her head on his shoulder and inhaling the dark scent of cedar and flames.

"I am sorry I didn't think to offer you a ward of protection before we went out tonight. I failed you." Marron leaned his head against hers as he whispered to her.

She lifted her head and met his deep blue eyes. "You did not fail. Marron, I was married to him. I know better than anyone what to expect from him. I was stupid to think I was safe. I need to find someone who can tattoo me. It's the only way to ward him off. If you three are going to stick around me, you should get protection spells tattooed on you as well."

Marron chuckled. "I already have one, as does Evan. You never know what you'll come across in battle. Meraena, well, I don't know about her. We will set something up with Evan's tattoo artist tomorrow."

"He once found my ward tattoo against demon possession and peeled it from my scalp. He thought I would end it there. I refused to reproduce with him. I knew what kind of spawn he would create. I called in a favor to Hecate and had her carve the protection ward into my hip bone. I had my midwife claim I needed to recover from a miscarriage."

Marron stared at Fenryn speechlessly. Finally, he wondered aloud, "Do you think that the ward is still there?"

"I don't know, honestly. My scars are all still there. I would imagine a ward carved into my bone would remain as well."

Marron caressed her back and leaned his forehead on hers. "I will not rush you, Ryn. The fates may have linked us, but the progress of our relationship will always be your call. I will follow your lead. And if you are never ready, then that is okay too."

"Marron…" She closed her eyes and dropped her forehead to his chest.

"I am aware of the consequences, princess. As are you, I'm sure. But I understand what you've been through far more than you realize. I refuse to be another man forcing himself upon you. You are free in this."

The consequences of choosing to ignore their bond were dire. At best, they would be rendered mortal. At worst, they would be fatally ill within a few short years. The decision, as always, was in the fates' weathered hands.

She sighed and laid her forehead back against his and closed her eyes.

Evan cleared his throat beside them. "You two may want to get a room or separate from each other. Your auras are quite literally radiating throughout the entire room."

Fenryn pulled back as far as Marron allowed – no more than an elbow's length – and peered around. Sure enough, the entire dance floor glowed violet, and the light seemed to cascade out of their chests. She looked to Marron and then back to Evan. Her mind was full of questions she couldn't form in words.

"I have never seen anything like this before." Evan pulled his hand through the light, which merely spread around his fingers.

"I have." Meraena smiled at Fenryn. "Persephone and Hades. The aura of their love is a neon pink color. When they are joined together, it's the most vibrant and beautiful thing. The entire underworld is encased in a hue of pink for the first week of their reunion."

Fenryn laughed as Marron held her to his chest.

"Evan, can you get her in for a protection ward at Vald's tomorrow?" Marron stroked Fenryn's hair and took in her body. She reminded herself that she was a badass Valkyrie warrior. It would be far beneath her to get weak in the knees for the first man to show her kindness, but damn if it didn't stir something deep inside her.

"He *will* take her. Then you and me, lady. We will fight with the berserkers tomorrow and try to coax your true form out. It's time we see the true beast within."

Fenryn offered a feral growl that sent everyone around her into hysterics.

"We'll work on that too." Evan patted her head and motioned to the bartender to pour them another round.

"I have a question." Fenryn drew away from Marron and looked at her three friends. "If you all are royals and a captain, how are you *not* getting bombarded with psychos all day? You all just walk around like it's nothing."

Meraena's grin was the most sinister expression Fenryn had ever witnessed on the mermaid. "Glamour."

Fenryn blinked. "Are you glamoured to me?"

"No. High fae know who we are regardless, but when it comes to mortal humans and lesser fae, our glamours make us appear as one of them," Marron explained. He tapped on her mental wall. When she dropped her guard, he showed her what they looked like to others. Evan was tall, with tan skin, light brown wavy hair, and brown eyes. Meraena had onyx curled hair and mocha skin. Marron was red-haired and fair-skinned. None of them resembled their true form, just a generic version of it.

"I need to learn how to do that, too." Fenryn grimaced at the thought of all the things she had forgotten, all she had yet to learn. Where had the former Valkyrie gone? Where was the woman who could once slay enemies or guard allies with unparalleled ferocity? Would she ever come back?

"I will teach you." Meraena hugged Fenryn's waist tightly and handed her a new drink. "Drink up. We've got a few more hours before they close shop.

That's when they play their best songs."

Marron watched Fenryn take a small sip of the cocktail.

It will take time, Ryn. Two hundred years trapped by a spell to protect your people is no small sacrifice. Relearning how to access your powers will take time.

We don't have the luxury of time, Marron!

He reached out for her hand silently. She stared at the offered hand and thought of what her acceptance might imply. Despite it all, she placed her hand in his.

The DJ began to play an upbeat melody and the couples lost themselves to the music. Meraena and Evan danced together in ways that proved their fluency in each other's body language. Marron's hands found Fenryn's hips as she danced, bringing her closer to him. He laid his chin on her shoulder and inhaled the scent of dark chocolate and citrus emanating from her. He gave into the desire to softly nip behind her ear. A soft moan escaped her lips.

Eventually Margot's did indeed close. The team exited the bar lighter than when they had entered.

"Tomorrow, princess." Evan threw a heavy arm over Meraena's shoulder. "We train in beast form. I'll meet you in Asgard at eight."

"Gods, Ev," Fenryn slurred with a laugh. "Not you too! I am not a princess. Loki is not a king! You're just fueling his ego. And if you can even make it out of bed by eight, I will meet you there." She waved to the couple.

Meraena ran out from under Evan and hugged Fenryn's waist. "We will destroy our enemies!"

Fenryn laughed and ruffled the mermaid's purple mess of hair. It had grown in volume from dancing and sweating. "As soon as we sober up."

"Bah!" Meraena shooed Fenryn's hand away and sauntered back to her mate. "See you tomorrow. I'm staying with my man tonight." All the sexual tension leaked out of that statement.

Marron shook his head, but a true smile crept across his face. "Don't forget protection!"

Evan flipped him off, which Marron returned with a grin.

"Ready, Ryn?" Marron extended a hand to the

remarkably lighthearted female.

"Are you taking me home, prince?" Fenryn linked her arm through his and headed towards the dark sidewalk, which was only lit by streetlights and the neon signs of closed shops.

"If you'll allow it."

"I believe I will." Fenryn chuckled. She leaned her head on his shoulder as they walked and gazed at the stars which seemed to follow them along their path.

"Thank you for tonight." She inhaled the night air, which had a light scent hinting at rain on the horizon. Freedom. The stars, darkness, and light; all of it screamed to her of freedom.

"Anytime, princess." His arm wrapped around her waist as they reached the apartment building.

"Will I see you at training tomorrow?" She stepped out from his arms and met his gaze.

"I *am* a shifter." He smirked, but the expression faltered. "I don't know. I need to try and smooth things over at home and see where everything lies with Kornelia and her family."

Fenryn pursed her lips and looked to the stars. "I didn't intend to uproot your life, Marron. I never wanted a mate, nor did I think I would find one."

A gentle calloused hand found her cheek and drew her attention back to the prince. "I am not sorry to have met you, Ryn. I think we are in for a wild ride together." With a wink and a lingering kiss on the cheek, Marron faded home.

Fenryn stood on the doorstep and stared at the space he once occupied in shock.

Get your sexy ass inside, princess.

She stuck her tongue out to the midnight air, earning a mental chuckle inside her mind. She faded to her bedroom, undressed, and slid between the satin sheets. She knew she should take a shower and wash the night off her skin, but she wasn't ready to part with certain moments from the night. Marron's hands roaming up her sides, gripping her hips as she danced against him, savoring the feel of him against her backside.

Fenryn's hand slid beneath the waistband of her shorts as she closed her eyes.

Fucking Hel, Fenryn. Put your shields up! I was in the middle of talking to my father. *Three hundred years old is a bit old for an impromptu boner.*

Her entire body caught fire with the blush of embarrassment. *I'd say sorry, but I don't know that I really am.*

By all means, he growled, *carry on. For both our sakes.*

Oh, I will, but this isn't how you get to see me climax for the first time. And with that she threw up her mental shields and felt Marron all but slam into them.

Laughing, she turned out the lights and tucked herself into bed.

MARRON

Sleep did not find him that night. Instead he was covered in a cold sweat, replaying the attack at Margot's. How could he have been naïve enough to think she would be safe, even in a place like Margot's? He should have been by her side, should have protected her better. The rage he had felt at the sight of the blood trickling down Fenryn's neck- She deserved better. He would kill Apopis. His mate's fear deserved to never live in fear again. She had been through enough. He would do better in the future. He had to.

CHAPTER 12

Her sleep was so sound and dreamless that only the pounding on her front door finally stirred her from bed.

"Damn it, princess," Evan shouted from the hallway. "You have Marron's balls in a wad. He can't reach you through your bond. Plus, you're an hour late for training. Apparently, calling Marron was the wrong first step…"

Fenryn opened the door groggily. "Good morning, general. You woke me up. Congratulations." She threw her sleep disheveled hair into a top knot. "I'll go change and be out in a moment."

"You have two minutes." Evan started a timer on his smart watch.

I'm fine. She sent down her telepathic bond as she dressed in black athletic tights and a maroon tank top.

You shielded yourself in your sleep. I was about to fade over there.

I'm leaving for Asgard now. Feel free to join us

in the shifting ring.

Will you bring your wolf?

Gods, I hope so.

She glanced in the mirror and made peace with her just-rolled-out-of-bed look. "I'm ready!" She beamed as she exited her room.

"Good," Evan grumbled and took her hand. They both faded to Asgard. "Meraena will be here in a few hours. One thing to know about that man of yours is that he's a chronic worrier. Maybe lower your shield when you're sleeping, or… Something. I haven't seen Marron so worried in at least a hundred years. Here." Evan shoved a cellphone into Fenryn's hand. "Marron all but ordered me to give you one of these, since your bond isn't enough. All our numbers are already saved in it."

Fenryn stuffed the phone into her pocket. "I didn't know my shield was still up. It wasn't intentional. He could have faded, though."

Evan removed his shirt and entered the ring. "He's meeting with Kornelia's family today. They are in the middle of negotiations for a peace treaty to be signed. He can't leave. Now shift."

The order sent a chill down Fenryn's spine. She stood straighter and searched for her inner wolf. A dark pit was all she found instead. ***Come on. Come out and play.***

No. Her wolf growled.

Fenryn balked at the firmness and chill coming from the reply in the void.

Please. Fenryn closed her eyes and begged the hidden beast.

He killed so many last time. My fault. My fault. He killed the babes. No. The wolf whimpered and held firm.

Fenryn froze as an unwelcome memory surged to the forefront of her mind.

"You will bow to me and yield your wings." Apopis towered over Fenryn, the pristine onyx skin of his chest bared. Pure muscle rippled down as he raised her Valkyrie sword. "You are no warrior here. You are here for one thing. You're here to bear children and bring Ra and his constituents to their knees with our reign."

"I earned my wings. I will never yield them, not to you nor to any other god. My father may have handed you my body, but he has not handed over my spirit to you."

Fire raged in Apopis' eyes. The blade slashed through the air faster than Fenryn could move. A scream raked through her body. She had never known she was capable of such rage. Her wings fell to the ground with a wet unnerving sound. Her wolf form immediately took over and raged.

She tore into his chest, determined to rip Apopis to shreds even as blood poured down her back. Apopis called on his demon army, unable to throw her wolf form off, intestines falling out of his putrid stomach.

"Chain the beast in iron! I will show this insolent bitch the price of disobedience. I am your master!"

Black misty hands wrapped around her legs and dragged her to the iron chains awaiting on the far wall. She bit and thrashed at the red eyes in the mist to no avail.

Apopis raised his golden scepter and healed his

wounds. He beckoned for twenty women and children slaves to be brought into the chamber. Their filthy clothes clung to their thin bodies in torn scraps. Dirt and blood covered their skin.

"You will never lay a hand on me again, stupid whore." Apopis spat at Fenryn. "Kill them all."

Her wolf form roared helplessly against the iron shackles. The black mist tore through every slave. Their screams of pain and horror echoed and replayed in her mind throughout the forty days she was left tied to the wall and chained in irons.

Fenryn shook with rage. Her attention came back to the mass cowering in the dark.

We hide no more! We have a team now. We will murder the Demon King. You and me. We will rip his head from his body and tear him limb from limb, but I need you to come back. I need to train with you now. And I need your help to kill him.

I failed. Her wolf whined.

No, you never failed. We were unevenly matched and ill-prepared for war. But we are ready now. We will win. Fenryn reassured her beast.

The wolf stepped slowly forward. She was massive and beautiful. Her fur was black as night, so black it blended into the void. But her green eyes shone bright.

Thank you. Fenryn smiled.

The wolf nodded.

Fenryn shifted into a thing of brilliance and terror with no further warning. She was larger than any berserker. Evan himself had to step back and assess the situation. He let out a low whistle and shifted into his berserker form.

First, he charged Fenryn with brute force. She batted him away with minimal effort.

"This is pathetic." Loki sighed, fading in at the far side of the sparring ring. He stalked forward radiating annoyance and disappointment. "You cannot train with a berserker. Your wolf form is nearly three times his size."

Fenryn snarled at her father and charged towards the god, who simply faded to the other side of the ring.

"Catch me, daughter. Make me pay for selling

you to the Demon King." Loki's eyes blazed with flame.

Fenryn charged Loki and missed him by a hair's breadth.

Loki roared. "Fade, child! You are so much more than this! Fade in wolf form! Catch! Me!"

Fenryn's hackles rose with a growl. She lowered herself to a pounce and focused on fading. Loki, who anticipated her actions, sidestepped quickly, though not quickly enough to avoid a swipe from Fenryn's claws.

"Better," Loki nodded and pulled at his torn sleeve. "Again."

Fenryn continued chasing her father. Once they mastered their game of cat and mouse, Loki removed his suit jacket, which was now nought but shreds. He rolled the sleeves of his button up shirt over his elbows.

"Now let's bring your fire into the mix." Loki stared his daughter down. "Come on. You must think I deserve to *burn*. Your mother certainly believes so. To be completely honest, neither of you are wrong."

Fenryn snarled and prowled towards the god. Her coat lit on fire. Her smoking paws seared the dirt with each step she took. She slipped into her female form unconsciously, now wearing her sports bra and leggings.

"He is destroying me!" Fenryn's shoulders shook with effort as she attempted to contain her silent tears.

"You are standing quite well for someone who claims to be broken." Loki tucked a sweat laden curl behind her ear.

"You have no clue, Loki!" She threw her sports bra off and turned to show her father the skin around her arm-covered breasts. "Iron in every gouge. I never healed. *Look* at where my wings were. He killed twenty innocent women and children in front of me that day. You don't *know!* You sold me to a monster!"

Loki reached out as if to touch the jagged scars in Fenryn's body. He could see that they were still capped by iron to prevent the wing from regrowing. "We didn't *know.* We were locked in Asgard. It wasn't until you made your deal with Hecate that we were released. We thought you had died."

"Well, I didn't die. I was just stuck in some

fucked-up shifter form. Safe from anyone ever discovering me. For two hundred years. Two hundred years, Dad! I didn't even know who I was!"

"The man I married you to was not Apopis. One of his demons in disguise was playing the part. I didn't know, Fenryn. I knew Apopis ruled over demons and fire but come on! So does Hades! Look at him and Persephone! It's not perfect, but it is love."

Fenryn studied the god. She could see the vulnerable brokenness on his face. She wasn't ready for this conversation. She wasn't ready to forgive him.

With a wave of his arm, Loki plunged the training field into a vision of the past.

Loki's warm dining hall was ablaze with preparations for winter solstice celebrations. The servants were bustling around the hearth, lining candles haphazardly as their laughter bubbled from their lips. Loki grinned as he tucked the flask of bourbon into his jacket. They'd all be passed out soon and he'd have Angrboda to himself.

He was in the middle of throwing back a shot of whiskey and picturing his wife's perfect ass naked and bent over the dining room table when Erik cleared his throat from the doorway.

"What?" Loki all but barked at his butler.

"There is a God Apopis at the door asking for an audience with you." Erik's face remained neutral. Whatever he thought of this God, he kept it hidden. Granted, Loki could break those walls, but he truly valued Erik and today was not the day to betray his trust.

Loki nodded, adjusting his elegant black and gold embossed tunic. His fur cloak billowed behind him as he strode to the receiving room.

Standing near the dining cart filled with cloud berries was a tall male dressed in pristine white and gold framed dress? Loki had never seen a male in such clothing.

"Shall I offer you a fur pelt? Winter is in full swing here in Asgard." He eyed the exposed tan skin of the male before him.

A rich chuckle rumbled in his throat. "I am well, thank you God Loki. I have come to ask for your daughter's hand in marriage."

Loki felt his eyes narrow as he scrutinized the God before him. His chestnut curls framed a chiseled, tan jaw line. The vibrant green eyes held Loki's stare.

"My daughter is a warrior, not a prize bride. Why would you wish for her hand?"

"I am the ruler of the Egyptian Underworld. I need a partner with an understanding in chaos and fire. Females like her are few and far between." Apopis crossed his arms over his chest, watching Loki with confidence.

Loki withdrew the flask from his cloak and took a long drag. "It would seem we have much to discuss, but I must insist you find proper clothing for our weather."

Fenryn studied her father for a long moment. The vision confirmed the male certainly wasn't the Apopis she knew. "I hear you, but I need time."

Loki cleared his throat and nodded as he grabbed his shredded jacket and faded out of the ring.

Evan shifted back into his male form and walked over to Fenryn. He handed her a shirt and sighed. "Yeah, he was right. I would not have known to push you like that."

Fenryn huffed and turned her back to Evan. She threw on her bra and Evan's shirt in a hurry. "Don't tell Marron you got to see my breasts."

"I don't have to tell Marron shit. He saw everything. He faded in once Loki crashed the training. He felt your energy shift."

She looked around the ring.

Those are remarkable breasts.

She turned abruptly and found Marron sitting atop of the fence frowning at her scars. He motioned for her to join him.

"We can get the iron out of your scars, Ryn." Marron stood as he approached her. "I didn't know it was still in there. You must be in pain all the time."

"It's been over two hundred years, Marron. The only thing I notice, is that I cannot regrow my wings."

Marron's frown deepened. He pulled Fenryn into his arms and wrapped her tight in his embrace.

She stiffened for a moment, until something within her gave way and all the heartbreak she felt finally unleashed itself. Fenryn clung to Marron's chest as if he were a lonely lifeboat in the middle of a raging sea. He held her and caressed her back as she cried into his chest.

"I couldn't save them. Those women and children. I didn't back down and they paid for my pride. It was my fault."

"You are not responsible for that monster's actions. You had no clue he would do that. No one did, Ryn. Now we know and we can plan accordingly." His hands found her face and lifted her gaze gently to his until their eyes met. "We will bring him and his demons down to their knees. Judging by your memory, Apopis was no match for your wolf form. We just need a plan to immobilize his demon army."

"You are quite a spy on my thoughts, Marron." She dropped her forehead on his chest, too exhausted to truly fight.

"I wanted to see your wolf form, but I didn't expect that memory to emerge. I am sorry for overstepping." He ran his hands up and down her back, raising goosebumps on her arms. "May I call my healer to remove the iron from your scars?"

"Do I even deserve my wings after everything that happened?" Fenryn sank to the ground and covered her face with her hands. "I should have fought harder!"

Marron sat next to her and took a deep breath. "I used to fight with the berserkers. Evan and I trained together as children. My father thought military training would benefit a future king. Evan led us to battle between Asgard and Mt. Olympus just before Odin's peace treaty was signed. We fought one single battle against Hephaestus. We were young recruits, too stupid to know the first thing about leading an army.

"Basically, Hephaestus made a laughingstock of our team and destroyed the city of Pompeii along the way. I'm sure you're familiar with the tale. Us brutes are nothing against a volcano. Everyone who couldn't fade away died. Evan got so dark after that. I thought for sure I'd lose him to suicide or a foolish decision in battle." Marron closed his eyes and took a deep breath. "Their screams still haunt me at times. The consequences of our decisions are something we learn day by day to live with, and we work through them as they present themselves. But you are worthy of living your life. Moreover, those slaves deserve to claim their revenge."

Fenryn sniffled ungraciously and looked up. "Did you ever get revenge on Hephaestus?"

"No. The treaty was signed before we could do anything like that. Besides, the lessons from that battle *had* to be learned."

Fenryn pondered Marron's words, not sure what to think of them. Her stomach growled, loud and demanding.

Marron laughed. "I think Meraena is ready for your glamour lessons. Do you think you can make it?"

She inhaled his scent of cedar and fire. "I have to."

He tipped her chin up to look at him. "You don't have to do anything, Ryn."

She gave him a small smile. "I'm ready."

"Good," Meraena chimed as she entered the ring. "Because we are blowing this popsicle stand. Let's get you a glamour and find a dress for the ball."

Fenryn laughed and gestured at her sweaty body. "I need to shower first."

"Want company?" Marron winked, a rogue smile playing on his lips.

She took in his form: his relaxed posture, the dark tattoos peeking out from the collar of his dress shirt. She swallowed. *Yes.* But she couldn't bring herself to admit it just yet. "No."

Marron dipped his chin. "Very well. I'll await your call, my lady."

Fenryn scrunched her nose and rolled her eyes. "Goodbye, Marron."

"Say my name again. I like it." His voice was husky with desire.

She blushed and offered a vulgar gesture in exchange before fading to her bathroom. She peeled off her clothes and dropped them to the floor with a wet *plop.* Then she stepped into the tub and reveled in the chill of the water's first stream.

CHAPTER 13

Fenryn replayed the training in her mind as she washed. She wanted to curse her father for crashing her training, but she knew Evan was right. It would have taken him far more time to figure out how to push her. She was trained by Tyr, not Loki. Tyr was the one to thank for her battle instincts, but her cunning, her anger, her stubbornness – all of those she inherited from Loki. He *knew* how to rile her up. It was effective. *Gods, I miss Tyr*, she thought. *He was a worthy opponent.*

Finally, clean scrubbed and smelling of rose petals, Fenryn shut the tap off and wrapped herself in one of Meraena's fluffy towels. She marveled at how soft towels had become over the past two hundred years. She dried her hair and threw on an olive-green lace dress with sheer black tights and black combat boots, a dagger hidden in her right boot.

She stared at herself in the mirror and frowned at her wet hair. She wondered if she could do something about it. She sent some of the heat from her flames into the air around her head. Shaking out her wet locks, everything was dry within seconds.

"Perfect," she smiled at her reflection with pride blooming on her lips.

She stepped out and met Meraena in the living room. "Alright, I am going to be honest. I have never glamoured before. I would imagine it's like shifting, right?"

Meraena laughed. "Kind of, except you want to stay in your fae form. Let's focus on the red hair. Imagine every strand of your hair turning red."

"Easy enough." Fenryn closed her eyes and pictured her hair turning red.

Meraena bit her lips and held back her laughter. "Maybe not that shade of red. You look like a clown."

Fenryn blanched as she looked at herself in the mirror. She looked like someone had colored her hair with a neon red crayon. She tried to imagine Marron's auburn hair and landed somewhere between natural ginger red and a deep scarlet color.

"I'll accept that." Meraena clapped and took a bite out of a chocolate chip cookie. "Now lighten your skin and add thousands of freckles."

Fenryn frowned. "Can I have an image for reference?"

"No, because then you'll end up looking like the model." Meraena motioned for her to continue.

Fenryn huffed and focused on the fairest shade of skin she could recall from the Norse fae. *Thousands of freckles, what does that even look like?* She thought to herself in confusion. *Were they evenly dispersed?* She decided to simply go with freckles within eyesight.

Meraena pursed her lips and studied her friend. "You look like a ghost with black spots. Give yourself more color. This would be a good Samhain costume though."

"People still practice that?" Fenryn asked as she darkened her skin pigment.

"Better." Meraena nodded. "Some do. All right, now to the dressmaker. The boutique which best fits your style is on the edge of Mt Olympus. I'll take us there. Your eyes still need to be gold, though."

Fenryn blinked and changed her eyes to gold.

"Eerie. Wonderful!" Meraena clapped and grabbed Fenryn's hand. They both faded to the doorway of a shop with a sign saying *Aurelia's Boutique.*

"Aurelia," Meraena called out from the front door. "It's Mer."

A tiny female with blonde hair tied neatly in a bun and wrapped in flexible measuring tape popped out from behind skeins of fabric. Fenryn noticed the pins lining the lapel of her miniscule vest. "Mer! I was wondering when you would bring your friend over."

"Here we are! Sorry, it's going to be a rush order. We need it ready in two days." Meraena's face radiated her sympathy.

"Bah, I do my best work on a deadline. Now, let me look at you." Aurelia waved Fenryn forward. "So tall! It's not every day I encounter a woman over six feet tall. I assume one of your parents is a giant."

"Keep your assumptions to yourself." Meraena's tone turned lethal.

"Always." Aurelia smiled widely. "Is this your natural style? Dark colors with lace and intrigue?"

"If that is how you'd describe it, then yes. This is the style I feel comfortable in." Fenryn watched the woman circle around her before climbing up a step ladder to grab measurements.

"Very well. I have what I need. Your ball gown will be ready for pickup in a day and a half. Now, begone! I need to get to work."

"You're the best, Aurelia!" Meraena blew the dressmaker a kiss.

Aurelia shooed her off cheerfully. Fenryn was left more confused than confident that her gown was taken care of.

"We didn't pay her." Fenryn began walking back.

"Marron already paid her, Ryn. It's taken care of. As is her silence."

Fenryn nodded. "When do I get to be myself again then?"

"Well, I know the prince wants a date with you tonight. Do you want to give him a test?"

Fenryn laughed. "He will know."

Meraena shrugged. "Maybe."

Fenryn let the thought play out. What would the prince do if a redhead with golden eyes approached him, flirting and…

And what, Ryn? What would this redhead do? Would she touch me? Would she be ballsy? Would she be shy and meek?

Damn it, Marron!

Shields up, princess, he said in a sing-song voice. *Also, you both forgot that I was there three hours ago when Mer gave you instructions. I would know it was you immediately.*

Rude. She rolled her eyes and followed Meraena into the nearby cafe.

Until you learn to glamour your scent, I will always know it's you, princess. Tell Mer I'm picking you up in forty-five minutes.

"Can you glamour your own scent?" Fenryn asked Meraena, who handed her an iced mocha. They began walking along the sidewalk, which was lined with tiny shops. "Also, we have forty-five minutes until Marron is here."

"I haven't ever tried masking my scent. I never

really thought about it, but it's worth trying. If you can do it, you've mastered fae glamour." Meraena took a long drink from her cup. "I don't know if you can hide your essence, though. Why don't you try it while we walk? Go for a cinnamon and lavender scent."

"Very specific." Fenryn laughed and brought her wrist to her nose. She breathed in her normal scent of chocolate and citrus. She willed it to turn into anything but that. She begged it to turn into cinnamon and lavender. Thirty minutes of concentration later, Fenryn was left with her original scent and a lukewarm coffee in her hand. She was defeated.

"Fade home, Ryn." Meraena laughed and patted her friend's arm. "Changing your scent is like changing the blood running through your veins. It might not be impossible, but it won't be accomplished in under an hour."

"Where will you go tonight?" Fenryn asked, watching Meraena finish off her latte.

"Evan and I have a sex date tonight." Meraena winked at Fenryn and faded away.

Fenryn shook her head and did the same thing.

She faded to their apartment and caught a final glimpse of the stranger in the mirror. She closed her eyes and willed herself back into her own skin, eyes, and hair. Then she changed into an evening gown for her date with Marron.

Ready. She sent down the bond with a smile.

Perfect. I'm outside your door.

Fenryn unlocked the bolt and found the prince leaning completely at ease against a wall on the other side of the door. He was dressed in a black suit with a dark jade tie, one leg propped against the wall, hands in his pockets. His long auburn hair framed his face. Her desire flamed hot and demanding at her core.

His burning gaze slowly trailed up from her boots to the rest of her body, pausing at the plunging neckline of her dress. When his eyes finally met her stare, his desire was just as evident.

"Dinner?" Her question was more of a rasp than actual words.

Marron pushed off the wall and offered Fenryn his arm. She took it and they immediately faded away. They landed in a secluded room in a bustling restaurant.

"Mt. Olympus." Marron explained as he pulled a chair out for Fenryn to sit in. "We are in Hecate's realm. I wanted an opportunity to thank her for helping you. We are in The Genevieve, the best restaurant in all of Mt. Olympus."

"You're just full of surprises." Fenryn put a cloth napkin in her lap as a pixie server flew into the room.

"Lady Fenryn?" The woman gasped. "I had heard rumors you had risen, but I did not believe them. It is an honor to serve you." Her hand rose to her glowing chest. "I apologize, Prince Marron." She rushed a curtsy to the prince. "I would not be here if not for your sacrifice all those years ago. My mother was able to flee the country because of your deal with Hecate. Many of us live here in Mt. Olympus now. She gave us sanctuary. My mother hung your portrait in our living room. We honor you every year on the day of your sacrifice."

Fenryn was speechless. Her blood ran cold as she took in the pixie's words. "My people. Were they truly able to reach safety? Did it work?"

The pixie smiled broadly, a yellow light expanding around her. "Yes, Lady. Hecate was able to hold off the demons while we escaped. From the stories my mother told us, the demons were imprisoned while you were lost to us."

"I am glad to know it all worked. I intend to keep Apopis from finding any of you ever again. I will continue defending you all. That is my promise to you and to our people." Fenryn stood up and bowed to the pixie.

The pixie's light turned pink. "I am no one to bow to, Lady, but I will share your message. Thank you, from all of us. What can I get you to drink?"

Fenryn and Marron ordered their drinks and were suddenly left sitting in awkward silence.

A gentle stroke on her mental wall provoked her to meet his gaze. She dropped her barriers and let him in.

What are you thinking, princess? Marron leaned forward and held her stare, propping his chin on his hands.

I should have stayed hidden as that shifted...

creature. Disgust filled her every word. *I know I didn't remember anything, not even who I was anymore... But what the Hel have I allowed to come back into the world now?*

Marron took her hand in his as wine poured into their glasses by an unseen hand. There was no sign of their pixie server anywhere.

Spells are never designed to last forever. Everything always comes to an end. Hecate is a strong enchantress, but she cannot hold the Demon King forever. You saved your people. You got them to safety. The cost was great, but you did it. Now it's time for the next step. We will prepare for the coming attack and strike Apopis hard and fast.

"I'm sorry to interrupt," the server whispered.

"It's no bother." Fenryn smiled at the pixie. "It's probably poor form to communicate without words in public anyways."

Marron scoffed. "I don't know if this private lounge counts as being in public, but Lady Fenryn is right. You are not interrupting us."

"Are you ready to order?"

Fenryn ordered a medium-rare steak in garlic butter with a side of sweet potato fries. Marron asked for a filet mignon and baked potato.

"How is Kornelia handling everything?" Fenryn asked, taking a sip of her wine.

"I think she is as relieved as I am, honestly. All her crying has stopped, she almost seems like a normal person now. It makes me wonder who she really is."

"Do you think a friendship could be formed between you once your peace treaty is signed?"

Marron took a long drink before answering. "I don't know. I need to know more about her and her family before I say yes to a friendship. But at least for now we won't be going to war against each other."

"That is always a plus." Fenryn chuckled, finishing her glass. It immediately refilled itself. "That is both wonderful and dangerous."

Marron smirked. "Just like you, princess."

"You're going to leave this restaurant wearing wine if you don't quit it with the princess talk, Marron."

"I don't think I will." He flashed her a wicked grin and a wink as he finished his own glass. "Because after dinner, *princess*, we are going to Asgard, where we will let our shifter forms out to play."

The low rumble of his voice made Fenryn cross her legs and narrow her eyes at the cocky prince. "If you think your beast can keep up, by all means, *prince.*"

Their food arrived and they ate in heated silence. That is, until Hecate walked through the restaurant's gilded doors.

"Gods, no wonder you two wanted a private room. Your scents would disturb the entire dining room. Fenryn, you look absolutely stunning as ever." Hecate ran a smooth hand down Fenryn's cheek. "Marron, you're welcome. But your gratitude is unnecessary. Fenryn and I fought together when we were part of the Valkyries. We were a team for many years. I came to her call every time. She was just a stubborn ass who waited for years before reaching out."

Marron studied Fenryn and Hecate together. "Blood-bound. You two swore blood oaths together."

"We were sisters. There was no separating us. We will be bound forever. It's a different bond than yours, of course. It's only opened when one of us calls upon the other, like a phone call."

Tears filled Fenryn's eyes. She stood so abruptly that her chair tipped backward and threw herself into Hecate's arms. When the women embraced each other, an iridescent golden light formed around them, pulsing like a living heartbeat. Marron watched as the embrace healed a part of Fenryn she hadn't even known was missing, a piece of herself she didn't even know to ask for.

Hecate stood as tall as Fenryn, her long chestnut hair flowing down to her abdomen. She was wearing a plum dress which flowed to the floor and was only held together by a black ribbon belt around her waist. Her silver eyes took in everything around her.

"Thank you for harboring my people. Thank you for all that you did for us. I can never repay you." Fenryn dropped to her knees and kneeled in front of the goddess.

"This was never a debt, Fenryn. You sacrificed yourself to save you and your people. You paid the cost of losing yourself for two hundred years." Hecate gently lifted her friend up from the ground. "Royalty does not kneel."

"I am no one, Hecate." Fenryn shook her head and wiped away her tears.

Your people would disagree. Marron began. *Who did you save?*

Fenryn glanced briefly at Marron before returning her attention to Hecate.

"You are the daughter of Loki, for gods' sake. You are not no one!" Silver and black smoke swirled around Hecate's ankles. She shooed it away with a wave of her hands. Her nose scrunched with disgust. "Enough of this. When do we get that iron out of her? I can smell it in her blood."

Marron blinked at Hecate. "I only found out today. I was going to arrange a meeting with my palace healer tomorrow."

"Bah." Hecate dismissed him with another wave of her hands. "I will take care of it. We need more protection tattoos, yes?"

Fenryn laughed. "Yes. I do."

"Very well." Hecate clapped her hands and the trio faded to Hecate's palace. Her study, to be precise.

The dark gothic ambiance of Hecate's personal space seemed at odds with her Greek heritage. The towering walls were ensconced in baroque wood furnishings and lined by books. A fire roared in the center of the room. It was surrounded by a black brick facade and framed by ferns draping from the mantle. A large window framed in gold glowed with bright starlight.

CHAPTER 14

Fenryn placed a gentle hand on Marron's shoulder. The prince was taking in his surroundings, trying not to be completely thrown off by the sudden change of plans.

"Lay down on the chaise." Hecate ordered.

Fenryn did as she was told. Hecate unzipped her dress and hissed at the brutal scars covering the other woman's back. "That son of a bitch will pay. We will bring him to his knees."

"*I* will bring him to his knees," Fenryn amended.

Hecate's fierce eyes softened. "Yes, you will. I am going to begin extracting the iron. It will be uncomfortable, but not painful. I am going to use magic, not surgical tools."

Marron came to Fenryn's side. "May I hold your hand?"

Fenryn laughed. "I believe this is the first time you have asked. Yes, you may." *My people,* she explained.

Were the thousands of slaves Apopis had hidden in his shadow realm. Slavery was outlawed long ago, but Apopis found a way to hide it. I didn't know the scale of it until what you saw in my memory. When I stayed in my wolf form so he would no longer rape me, he brought females in for me to watch as I was chained to the wall.

Her body shuddered at the memory. Silent tears fell to the chaise.

He would always leave the dungeon saying someone had to bear his demon heirs.

Marron took Fenryn's hand in his own as Hecate began her work. Fenryn hissed and bit her bottom lip. The procedure felt like it took hours. Beads of sweat formed on Hecate's forehead. She spoke words in an unfamiliar language over Fenryn and extended her hands over the scars. Tears escaped Fenryn's eyes as the last of the iron was finally removed.

Hecate dropped to the floor gracelessly and wiped her forehead. "Let's not wait two hundred years next time."

Fenryn tried to laugh, but it came out as more of

a huff. "Deal."

"Kornelia." Marron suddenly gasped. He looked like he just had an epiphany.

Hecate laughed and leaned back on her elbows, looking up to the ceiling. "Well done, prince. She is indeed here. We are mates. Her scent is everywhere. I glamoured our bond when her father arranged the marriage to you. I intended to approach you soon, to call off the marriage due to our bond, but I knew my spell on Fenryn was fading." Hecate stood and wiped her hands on the black silk of her pleated pants.

"I reached out to the Egyptian embassy when you returned. I believe Ra, the head of the council, has dealt with Apopis in the past. Hopefully, I will receive more information soon. I could feel Fenryn's power growing. I searched the realms tirelessly for her. She must have faded while she was the creature after a while because I had her here with me for the first fifty years. I didn't know where she was, but my spell told me she was safe. I had no clue you and Fenryn would be mates as well. The fates sure do enjoy a good laugh at our expense."

Fenryn lost all composure and laughed until her belly hurt. Soon, all three were laughing so hard that Kornelia came into the study to see what caused the commotion. She found the three of them in such a state that she sat with them on the floor until they calmed down enough to explain what in the underworld was going on.

"Are you going to regrow your wings?" Kornelia asked Fenryn tenderly once they all caught their breath.

"I don't know." Fenryn admitted, staring somberly at the scars on her wrists. "I am no longer a Valkyrie. I may have earned my blades back, but sporting their wings seems wrong somehow."

Marron ran his hand on hers. She met his gentle gaze and allowed herself to lean into him, savoring the comfort he brought her.

"Let me place the protection ward on you now that your back is healed." Hecate set her hand on Fenryn's right shoulder blade and uttered the incantation.

A swirling band of stars and crosses appeared in

the air, preventing possession and harm from demons.

"Thank you." Fenryn hugged Hecate. "For all you have done and everything you've given me."

"Thank you. For all you have done and will continue to do. Your people are lucky to have you, Ryn." Hecate kissed her cheek. "Now, go kick your mate's ass in the shifter ring. And make sure someone takes videos of it, please."

Marron raised a brow, "You think you're up for the challenge, Ryn?"

"Are *you*?" Fenryn countered and stood up. She turned her back to the prince so he could zip her dress back up.

Marron obliged and took her hand. He saluted Hecate, who had thrown an arm around Kornelia, then faded to Asgard with Fenryn.

"Show me yours, Prince and I will show you mine." Fenryn crossed her arms and leaned against the wall of the sparring ring.

"Very well." Marron smirked and removed his suit jacket, then followed by loosening his tie. Fenryn tracked every movement, especially as he began unbuttoning his dress shirt, revealing a perfectly sculpted body beneath. Norse and Greek tattoos woven for luck in battle were spread across his chest. Tattoos for losses marked on his left shoulder. The tree of life was inked on his right. "Not all of us have the magic to keep our clothes when we shift. Be warned that my pants are coming off next, princess."

A blush flooded Fenryn's cheeks. She turned around quickly. "Is it just the Asgardian clothes that are spelled then? The berserkers always return in their clothes."

Marron chuckled. "Yes, and my mother didn't know I was a shifter until I was too old to have a witch imbue my blood with the spell to keep my clothing safe."

It was through their bond that he informed her, *I'm ready. Come play with me, Ryn.*

She turned and beheld a massive wolf. In fact, the beast was probably her equal in size. He was massive, easily twice the size of Evan's berserker form, but his fur was white. His eyes held true in his wolf form, as blue as the tide of Poseidon's treasured waters.

Fenryn reached out and ran her hands along Marron's muzzle, awed by the beast in front of her.

Not quite the play I had in mind, princess.

Hush, you. Your beast is beautiful. I am admiring you.

Well, then, by all means. Marron's wolf lowered its head to her.

Fenryn rolled her eyes and sighed.

Well, are you ready? She asked her wolf.

Her wolf met her with eager eyes.

Very well, then. Fenryn smiled as she shifted and launched herself at Marron with no pause for decorum.

So that's how we are going to play? Marron's wolf snarled.

Fenryn bared her teeth towards him. Her hackles were raised, and her shoulders hunched as if ready to lunge forward. Marron rushed forward. Fenryn faded and attacked him from behind. He let out a howl of surprise and clamped his jaw around her shoulders. She yelped and dropped to the ground, rolling on top of him. He growled and faded away, reappearing directly on top of her and pinning her to the ground. Fenryn snarled and coated her fur in flames. Marron jumped off and huffed at her. Fenryn offered him her best wolfish grin.

Never forget that you can light yourself on fire, Ryn. Use it every chance you get.

Aye aye, Captain.

Marron's beast rolled its eyes.

Turn around, unless you wish to see me naked.

And what if I do?

Marron's eyes blazed. *Then* watch, *princess.*

He began to shift back to his human form. Fenryn wanted to watch every last second of it, but she lost her nerve and shifted back too... Now facing opposite of Marron.

Chicken, Marron teased.

"I'm dressed now."

Fenryn turned around. Marron was most definitely not dressed at all.

"Oh my Gods!" Fenryn covered her eyes. "Marron! Damn it!"

"I was just giving you what you were shouting down the bond. You might want to throw those mental shields back up, sweetheart."

She snarled, still covering her eyes, but threw her shields up immediately.

"*Now* I'm dressed." Marron laughed and stepped into Fenryn's space. "But if you ever wish for that not to be the case-" He trailed a finger lightly down her cheek. Fenryn's blush stained her skin and revealed the effect of Marron's words. "All you have to do is ask. Or take them off yourself." With a devilish wink, he faded away.

Fenryn shouted through the bond with a frustrated – albeit childish – stomp. *Damn it, Marron! Where the hell did you go?*

All part of our training tonight, princess. Follow me.

She looked around the abandoned training fields. The wind blew lazily through the trees and grass. The stars danced uninhibitedly in the night sky. Nothing hinted towards Marron's location. Fenryn threw her hands in the air and cursed the prince internally, demanding: *how?*

Our bond. Each fade leaves behind the essence

of the fader for a few minutes. Yours is of course an emerald aura. I do believe mine is royal blue, but you often call it sapphire in your mind. Look for that in the ether.

Fenryn huffed and turned her attention to the auras around her. She noted the pure white lining around all natural living things such as plants and trees. The small bugs flying in the night glowed with a faint lime-green hue. She searched for a color that spoke of Marron's presence. Indeed, there was a deep blue trail leading away. She faded slowly, following it to… Her bedroom.

She threw her hands on her hips. "You are such a man. Get out."

But Marron's face was too solemn for a mere game. He held up a hand to her, causing her to pause. "No. You aren't staying here. Neither is Meraena. We need to leave, now."

Fenryn assessed her room quickly. She noted an unwelcome scent that sent adrenaline surging through her veins. "How?"

"He's getting stronger. Just as you are." Marron

grabbed her hand and they faded away to an unfamiliar apartment.

CHAPTER 15

"Dammit, Marron. A knock or a warning next time would be great," Evan barked as he threw a blanket over a half-naked Meraena.

"Hey, Ryn." Meraena smiled and waved to her friend as she caught the blanket and covered her chest.

"He was in their apartment," Marron growled.

"Fuck." Evan ran his hand through his long hair and grabbed his shirt from the floor. "Alright. Asgard or Mount Olympus?"

"Hecate will take us in, but if we go there all my people will be discovered and targeted. He knows how to track me now. I won't put them at greater risk." Fenryn wrapped her hands around the burns on her wrists. "My father would take me in, but we would be quickly discovered there. Same with Marron's palace."

Meraena grabbed her dress from the floor and shimmied it over her body. "Perhaps it's time," she wondered aloud. "The ball is in two days' time. You know Apopis would be interested in crashing the ball. You might as well make it official and go to Marron's palace. Control the battlefield."

Marron stiffened and looked at Fenryn. "My father. I haven't prepared you for any of it. For everything you'll see when you meet him and my mother. Their opinion of Asgardians… It's against the law to beat your children now, but if I'd told him, you were my mate a hundred years ago?" Marron shook his head. "Fenryn, I am sorry for how they'll treat you at my palace."

"I guarantee I've experienced worse. I can handle resentment. Very well then." She lifted her chin with a deep breath. "Someone needs to get my things. And Meraena's as well, I assume."

"We will go." Evan gestured to himself and Marron. "Wait for us here."

The men faded and Meraena dropped to the couch. "I am *so* ready for a good battle. I haven't gotten to kill someone in so long, and sex really does nothing to alleviate the bloodlust."

"You're a siren? Not just a mermaid?" Fenryn took in her friend.

"Half. I am half-siren. My mother was the first

siren. I may as well be full siren with how strong her blood flows in my veins. I try very hard to ignore the bloodlust, but I would be lying if I said war doesn't sing to me like a long-lost lover."

"I am sorry. I can't even imagine."

Meraena shrugged. "Working with the Valkyries helps. They understand. When the bloodlust gets overwhelming, they give me a mission and it... it helps."

"I think the Valkyries have saved a great many of us."

"Indeed."

Marron and Evan returned; their arms laden with bags.

"Meraena, are you staying here with the Valkyries or the seas?" Evan leveled his mate with a stare and dared her to say anywhere but with him.

She rolled her eyes. "Wherever you go, I go, Ev."

"Damn right." He dropped her bags and kissed the top of her lavender curls.

"Let's go." Fenryn placed a hand on Marron's

shoulder. "Meraena's getting a bit chompy."

Meraena smiled, revealing a mouthful of dripping fangs.

"Gods, that is still nightmare-inducing." Marron shuddered as they faded just outside of his palace.

***

Gold. Everything around her was gold. The gates, the flags, the crests, the shutters adorning the windows, the curtains – it was all gold. A thin metallic layer lay around everything around her.

"How?"

"It is my father's curse." Marron stepped to the gates, which opened for him immediately. "I am so sorry in advance."

Fenryn brushed her hand against his. "I'll be fine."

"You may be," he grumbled, adjusting his suit, and running a hand through his auburn hair.

"You look great."

He chuckled and nodded. "As do you, princess."

The palace doors swung open. A petite woman clad in a golden gown with flowers blooming across the bodice and gray wind-swept hair ran towards them. She took the prince's face in her hands and exclaimed, "Marron, thank Zeus! You're back."

"Hello, Mother." He offered a genuine smile. "This is Fenryn, daughter of Loki. Fenryn, this is my mother, Queen Damodice."

The queen bowed her head to Fenryn. "A pleasure to meet you, my dear. Marron, I do fear your father is in a bit of a state. We need to get inside. You are most welcome here, Fenryn."

"Thank you." Fenryn offered a low curtsy and followed Marron and the Queen into the cold golden palace.

The entryway was dark, all light absorbed by the golden walls and floor. Fenryn tried to make out the old pattern that must have been etched there centuries ago, but the gold plating had eaten it away. This palace was more a cavern than a home, cold and foreboding.

A gentle, blue-colored nudge pressed against her mental shields. Fenryn glanced at Marron and dropped them momentarily.

I am so sorry for what you will see in the throne

room. Midas… He is unwell. It's the effect of his curse, as well as his general disposition. It's not an excuse, but… I'm sorry.

Fenryn turned to the grand doors. They were once undoubtedly made of wood and adorned with intricate metal fixtures. Now, they were just another icy fixture in this endless tomb of gold. It took four guards to pull the doors open.

Indeed, Fenryn was unprepared for the sight ahead of her. The first thing she saw was Midas himself. The old, withered man who sat on the throne was skin and bones. Wisps of gray hair fell down his shoulders. His eyes barely fluttered open, so heavy from the weight of his sagging eyelids. A golden gown covered Midas's body, yet it looked soiled, like he struggled to remove his clothing. A spiked crown of gold rested lopsidedly on his age-spotted head.

But it was what lined the walls of the throne room that caused Fenryn's dinner to rush up to her throat. A neat row of tiny infants was set to the King's left. They were all solid gold and no bigger than a cantaloupe.

They could not conceive, Marron supplied.

But then...? Fenryn shuddered as she took in all the bodies lining the room.

Marron cut her a glance that clearly warned her this was not the place for this conversation.

The king's gravelly voice broke the silence. "Is there a reason," he croaked, "that Asgardian forces requested to camp outside our territory for the next three days?"

"Yes, your Grace." Marron bowed his head to his father. "May I begin by introducing Fenryn Laufeyson, daughter of Loki. She sacrificed herself to save her people from her ex-husband, the Egyptian Demon King Apopis. She was locked in the shapeless form of a broken shifter for two hundred years. Now that she awoke and has regained her powers, we believe Apopis is also growing stronger. We anticipate he will attempt to make an appearance at the ball we are hosting."

The king frowned as he studied Fenryn. "Are you even worth it, child?"

"Of course –" Marron started to defend her.

"I did not ask *you*!" The king bellowed, holding up a silencing hand towards Marron. Fenryn looked beyond the hand and beheld a horrifying sight on the other wall. It was lined with hundreds of people who had likely spoken out against Midas as Marron just did. People he then turned to golden statements of his power.

"I do not expect you to believe I am worthy of defense, King Midas." Fenryn began, back straight, chin up, hands clasped behind her back, mental shields up. "However, my people, the citizens of Phrygia, deserve protection from the destruction Apopis' wrath will bring. I have seen him wipe out entire cities with a single word for refusing his tithe. He lives for the thrill of doling out punishment. Peace and coexistence are not part of his vocabulary."

"What makes you think peace is attainable?" Midas coughed openly, spit landing on the dais around him. "The treaty was signed one hundred years ago, yet the bickering continues."

"Bickering is far more amenable than war, I wager. The fates' meddling suggests that coexistence is more attainable, especially considering the bonded mates they paired in recent years."

"Ah yes, you and your bonded mates. How fortunate," The king sneered, acid coating his words. "The fates only choose ten every fifty years. Yet here my son stands beside the Asgardian filth he claims as his mate."

The fire in Fenryn's veins threatened to boil over. She wanted to demonstrate for Midas how filthy she truly could be. She took a deep breath and willed the ether around her and Marron to disperse, revealing their violet-colored mated bond.

"It is no *claim*, King Midas." Fenryn held his stare. "The fates have marked us."

Marron placed a hand on her shoulder. "Loki has placed his soldiers at the border with my permission. He is under strict orders to stay there unless Apopis enters Phrygia. Then and only then my he and his legion of berserkers enter. If they do pass through the border, they may only harm Apopis and his army. Any breach in this pact will result in Ares imprisoning them immediately."

Fenryn stared at the man beside her. Pride radiated through her chest. She understood well what game he was trying to win against Loki. Marron was trying to foresee and forestall all possible loopholes Loki could find in a binding contract.

King Midas assessed his son and waved a hand in dismissal.

Marron bowed low. Fenryn fought an inner grimace screaming to be let loose. Instead, she curtsied to acknowledge the dismissal. Queen Damodice ushered them out the door and sighed in what Fenryn assumed was relief.

"I got your message earlier, Marron. The room next to yours is ready for Fenryn. I have done all I can on my end." The queen looked Fenryn up and down. Fenryn was unsure whether her expression was one of concern or discernment, but at least it wasn't the disdain that filled Midas' heart. "Guard yourself, child. I doubt this fortress is much better than where you were before."

Fenryn dipped her chin. "Thank you, your majesty. I appreciate your time and effort. I apologize for all its inconvenience."

The Queen's jaw ticked. Fenryn could see that Marron had inherited her eyes' shape and color. Likely planned by the fates to protect the prince from accusations of being bastard born. Though Damodice's face was worn from age, it still retained a softness which reminded Fenryn of her own mother. Somehow this woman had withstood Midas's every cruelty and remained whole. That bravery alone deserved respect. "The fates play their own games. Midas plays his. If you ask me, it's all a giant chessboard. If we queens stand, all will be well."

Fenryn couldn't help the smile that bloomed on her lips at that statement. "Quite right."

Queen Damodice nodded at them both and kissed Marron on his cheek, before returning to the throne room once more.

CHAPTER 16

A soft caress slid down her mental barrier. Fenryn looked at Marron.

He waited.

Yes? She lifted an eyebrow.

Marron tilted his head towards the hallway and began walking.

Come on, princess. My room is this way. I am sure you are full of questions after that encounter.

I have a few. The first being, how is your mother not a statue like all the others?

Marron walked down the gilded hallway, which was somehow still dark and looming. A few lights lit the ominous expanse, but all they revealed was more gold upon gold. Marron stopped at the only wooden door Fenryn had seen so far. Protection spells and wards in wrought iron covered every inch of the door, similar to the tattoos on Marron's chest and forearms. The door sighed open as he placed a hand on it, shining with a brilliant blue hue.

My mother was imbued with a protection spell

upon her betrothal to Midas, for procreation. However, the witch that performed the spell could not protect the unborn children from being turned into gold.

Fenryn paused at the grand, yet out of place, room in the castle. The floors were a dark cherry wood with an ornate ruby-hued rug in its center. A cobblestone fireplace crackled with a lively blaze. The grand bed had been neatly made with summer-green duvet made of satin. There wasn't a single touch of gold to be found in Marron's apartment.

And you? How do you fit into this?

Into Midas's gift? I am a miracle." His smirk lacked true emotion. *"Honestly? My mother had an affair with Mars. She hoped her pregnancy would convince Midas to stop trying for another child. Once I was born, she had a midwife claim her uterus was ruptured and she could no longer bear children.*

Fenryn walked to the fire. She gazed at the flames as they licked the hearth and reached out to absorb some of its heat. *That was quite a risk to take. I know little of Mars, but I doubt he looks much like Midas.*

I am glamoured to look like him, but that glamour only works on him. I don't know the witch who cast that glamour. It was set by Mars, and as far as I know it was a transaction with Damodice, nothing more.

It is fortunate that you have her eyes…I wonder what he got from the deal.

Marron joined her by the fire, reaching out to warm his hands. *I never had the gall to ask.*

Fenryn turned towards the prince, her long hair falling over her shoulder as she moved. "The alliance you signed with my father. How many loopholes did you prepare for?"

"Up to and including stealing you. There are so many war crimes there, I had to consult with Ares before I sent it to be sure some of them could actually count." Marron smirked and took a deep breath. "I don't know if we can truly prepare for Apopis. Part of me wants to charge into his realm now, but that would be suicide. Another part of me believes that having the advantage of our home turf will serve us well, if he chooses to strike here."

I should just go back to him. The thought was too frightening for the words to leave her lips.

"Then what would everything you gave up have been for, Fenryn?" Marron reached out and cupped her smooth cheek in his rough hand.

I am a coward, letting you all fight for me when it's me that he wants. I could stop this. She dropped her head onto his shoulder.

To what end? And once he has you, what will his next conquest be? It won't be enough for him. One win isn't enough for a God like him.

Silence fell upon them for a long time as they sat together and watched the fire dance along the bricks.

Can we go for a run? She lifted her head and pleaded the prince with tearful eyes.

He laughed. "Of course, but you may want to change out of your dress."

"Oh, it's my wolf who needs to be let out, not me." Fenryn could feel her wolf clawing at her chest to break free. Too much, there was too much going on around her and the beast needed to be free, if only for an hour.

"Ah, yes." Marron held Fenryn's stare for a moment before placing a hand on her chest. "Mine gets restless too."

Fenryn's wolf stilled momentarily. The blue light seeped inward and calmed the racing urge to claw out of the confines of Fenryn's body. She swallowed and leaned unintentionally forward into the calming warmth that all but called and beckoned her home.

Marron kissed the tip of her nose and faded them away into a dense forest.

Be free, Fenryn.

That was all she needed to hear before the wolf leapt free and ran. She weaved in and out of the trees, breathing in the crisp smell of pine and earth and flowing water off in the distance. It was that scent she tracked. She trained every one of her senses on it. The trickling of the water against the pebbles along the bank, steam rising into the air preparing for the morning dew, frogs croaking inharmoniously. Finally, winded and at peace, she leapt into the river and dropped completely into the brisk, biting water, closing her mind to the world and the cold.

Oh, dear child, how you have grown. Tyr's voice echoed in the wind.

Tears slid down her cheeks. *I miss you.*

And I you, but the fates called me home. I am at peace, and you are exactly where you need to be, Tyr assured her.

I never got to apologize. I wasn't myself when I took your arm. I wasn't in my right mind at all. I had no control. My chains were imbued with magic.

Wind stroked her fur. *Sweet girl, I have always known that. I raised you and trained you. You think I wouldn't know when your wolf was gone?*

I love you, she cried.

And I you. All will be right.

She took a shuddering breath and let her body return to its natural form, her hands rising and falling in the river's current.

"Ryn," Marron's voice strained.

"Hmm?" Her eyes were still closed as she focused on the cool water sliding over her arms, core, legs, and feet.

"If you plan on torturing me, could you at least

give me a warning in advance?"

"What on earth are you going on about?" Fenryn opened her eyes only to see her shredded clothes floating down the stream. In her haste to let her wolf free she forgot to magically protect her clothes. She was laying before Marron absolutely bare. Water caressed every inch of her body.

"Oh my gods!" She immediately shifted back into her wolf form.

Marron laughed and threw off all his clothes, blessing her with a truly glorious sight. Tattoos wrapped around his shoulders, wards against evil and possession. Chiseled muscles defined his chest and abdomen, leading Fenryn's eyes further south. She should have turned, should have looked away, but she didn't. They were even now.

Even indeed. Marron chuckled down the bond. *Care to play, Ryn?*

Race you back! She darted away from the prince in a blur of dark fur in the night.

Meet you back in my room, Ryn. The dare in his voice sent a thrill down her spine she had no intent of ignoring. Fenryn ran until her legs wore out and she realized she could fade away.

Still naked, she faded into the prince's suite. "That was not a fair race." Her hands shot to her hips as she stomped in frustration.

Hunger flashed in Marron's eyes as he watched her breasts bounce in the air. "No one said I played fair."

He stalked towards Fenryn, nude as well. Heat burned within her.

"Marron." She didn't know if she said his name as a warning to herself or to him.

He continued approaching until her back pressed against the wall. His hand gently cupped her jaw, while the other rested just above her head. His body leaned in, dangerously close to touching hers in all the right places. Fenryn's hips betrayed her and canted towards him. Her chin lifted to meet his lips.

Marron grinned down at the beautiful female beneath him. Their bodies were on full display for one another, but neither one dared take their eyes off the other's.

"Yes, princess?"

She growled half-heartedly.

Marron leaned down and brought his lips to her neck. He kissed the tender skin behind her pointed ear and inhaled the intoxicating scent of dark chocolate and citrus.

A small moan escaped Fenryn's lips as she grabbed Marron's back and stroked his strong tattoo-covered muscles. Marron continued his perusal of her neck, scattering a mixture of nips and kisses down before dropping lower. He trailed tender, seductive kisses down her chest and over each breast, pausing to lick and suck each nipple. Fenryn gasped, her back arching off the wall.

Marron grinned before continuing down lower. His hands now slid down her body to the sides of her waist until the man knelt on his knees before her.

Spread your legs, Ryn. Marron looked up and waited for Fenryn to acknowledge her willingness, but she could see the raw desire blazing in his sapphire eyes. She could not bring herself to argue with him.

So, she spread her legs and gasped as his hot

tongue met her needy center. With a strong hand splayed on her abdomen and another on her thigh, Fenryn surrendered to the bliss of Marron on his knees. Gods. She had never been brought to feel this way with a man's tongue, utterly wrecked and fully worshiped.

Fenryn shouted his name as her entire body tensed up. She could have sworn she saw stars light the room as she found her climax and came to.

Marron grinned at her, pride written on his face, until Fenryn slid her hand slowly up his thigh. "I am not the only one who will get off tonight, Marron." Her hand met its mark and Marron groaned and leaned into Fenryn, gently biting the nape of her neck.

Fenryn dropped to her knees and winked at him. "Careful, prince. There is no wall to hold you up." With that, she took the prince in her mouth.

"*Fuck.*"

She wasn't able to give much of a demonstration before the prince withdrew. His hand laced through her long dark hair.

A knock sounded on Marron's door.

"Go away!" His voice broke as he roared at the

intrusion.

"Prince Marron," a servant spoke from beyond the door. "General Evan and Princess Meraena are at the door. They seem to believe you had plans to meet this evening."

Fenryn stood and stifled a fit of laughter. Marron dropped his forehead to Fenryn's and growled in frustration. Fenryn lost the battle and burst into laughter as she stepped away from the prince.

"This," Marron declared as he pointed to their naked bodies, his stormy eyes hungry with desire and braided russet hair askew, "this is not over."

She laughed again and ran a finger down his cheek. "Let's prepare for war."
Marron grumbled something unintelligible and threw on some clothes. Fenryn retrieved her own clothes from a bag Marron had packed for her in advance. Marron held the door open for Fenryn as they left his room. Giving him a ridiculous curtsey, she followed the prince to his private study.

CHAPTER 17

The team planned the ball over an early morning breakfast. They determined that the best location for the ball would be outside in King Midas's courtyard, for better access should Loki's soldiers be needed. Evan's berserkers will be stationed nearby, awaiting his signal. Hecate let them know there was still no word from the Egyptian embassy, but added she would travel there in person to persuade them. Marron's soldiers would guard every inch of King Midas's fortress. Marron, Meraena and Fenryn decided to ask for Loki's help to glamour the army battalions with invisibility.

"I am working on getting a squadron of sirens to aid us as well," Meraena chimed in around a steaming cup of coffee. "So far there are only fifty of us, but we are battle-trained for sea, should war ever come to Poseidon. The sirens know what you have done for the slaves of Apopis, Fenryn. They will support you."

Someday, princess, I want to hear the full story behind that. But only when you are ready to share it.

I am not proud of it, Marron. I could not save

everyone. I watched him kill and murder so many people while I was chained and powerless. They deserved so much better. I couldn't do anything.

Marron's tender eyes met hers. He placed a gentle hand on top of hers. *War brings casualties.*

She frowned and picked up a scone from the table. "Meraena, would you be willing to spar with me today? I think I could stand to learn some things about fighting someone half my size."

Evan laughed. "She's a prideful terror." He pulled his mate in and kissed the top of her curls.

Meraena's grin was all fangs. "I would love nothing more, Fenryn. But first, I must nap."

The two couples agreed to meet up around noon and departed. Marron led Fenryn back to his room.

Fenryn climbed into Marron's plush bed and was surprised as Marron pulled her tight against his chest. "You do know it's like 7 a.m., right?" Fenryn asked. "We're not going to have any time to sleep."

"Shush," Marron covered her mouth with his large, calloused hand. "I am trying to sleep."

Fenryn rolled her eyes and sunk into his body's

warmth. Bit by bit, she gave way to the lull of his deep breaths and firm chest behind her.

***

Servants began bustling around the hallway a few hours later. Fenryn stirred in Marron's sleep-heavy arms.

"Tell me about yourself, Marron. You know so much about me by necessity. We are to be mated and yet I feel like I barely know you."

The prince gently pushed dark locks away from Fenryn's face. He traced light fingers over the few freckles scattered across the bridge of her nose and observed the way the morning sun danced in her vibrant eyes.

"Well, I've been trained for the throne since birth," Marron replied. "My mother was tender towards me. I think some part of her regrets bringing me into Midas's house with him as my father. So many spells and protections have been placed on and around me. I got my first tattoo as an infant to ward against Midas' curse. When I was ten, I shifted for the first time. My father arranged to send me to Asgard to train with the berserkers. He believed them to be superior in combat over the legions of Mount Olympus.

"I stayed there for the next one hundred fifty years. I fought beside Evan as Asgard, Mount Olympus and Earth set up portals, fought over Scynthia and eventually developed what they hoped would be a long-lasting peace treaty."

Fenryn nodded. She vaguely knew about the portals created to make humans feel equal. Humans were given passes that allowed them limited access to the portals a certain amount of times a year.

Fenryn lifted her head from his bare chest. "Do you think the peace will last?"

Marron met her eyes and answered honestly. "I think there are too many moving pieces on the board for true peace to ever arrive. It's a noble goal. But there are too many kings and too many gods itching to stir things up. I don't count on the treaty holding for too long."

Fenryn laid her head back down and traced the tattoos enveloping Marron's chest. "I want to return to Asgard today and speak with the Valkyries. Brynhildr and I have a long-overdue talk."

"Do you want company?" His hand stroked her spine in a steady rhythm.

She shook her head and placed a tender kiss on his cheek. "I want to do this on my own."

Marron brought his nose to her jaw, placing tender kisses against her skin. Fenryn's eyes closed as she turned into him, gripping his strong shoulders.

The kisses quickly turned to nips as he made his way down her body, stopping to suck on each of her nipples until her back arched and her body demanded more.

"You are perfection, Ryn," he murmured against the sensitive skin of her hips, just as his teeth bit down on the hem of her underwear, pulling the obstacle down.

Her fingers wove into his thick hair and she gasped as his tongue brushed against her wanting center. "Marron."

He growled against her as he teasingly bit the bundle of nerves between her legs. Marron gripped her legs firmly, keeping them open before sliding a strong finger inside her.

"So wet and wanting for me, princess." Marron winked at his writhing mate as he worked her to the cusp of a world-shattering climax.

"Marron, please." She panted as he continued to stroke his finger along her inner walls, teasing.

"Please what, princess?" Marron took her nipple between his teeth and sucked.

"Quit playing and fuck me." Her voice broke with uneven breath.

"All you had to do was ask." Marron chuckled and replaced his finger with what Fenryn could only describe as heaven.

She could not be held responsible for the way her body responded to his as he moved with precision. The way her fingers dug into the skin of his back, there would certainly be blood. However, if he cared, he made no indication as he pinned her arms above her head. Marron drove Fenryn near madness with the intensity of the orgasm that consumed her body. They both lay in sweat-soaked silence after Marron came. Their ragged breathing was the only sound in the room.

After she regained her composure, Fenryn

placed a delicate kiss on Marron's forehead. "I should get going."

Marron nodded and watched as she rolled out of bed and dressed in her Valkyrie leathers, strapped her sword to her back and laced up her boots.

"Lethal," he growled, leaning towards her on the bed.

She smirked and took a deep breath, steadying herself. If she wasn't careful, she'd crawl right back into bed and pretend their problems didn't exist. "I'll see you tonight."

"I look forward to it." Marron's apprehension was palpable. Fenryn swallowed hard as she faded away from the naked man the fates decreed as her mate. She didn't deserve something so close to a blessing. She shielded her mind from Marron and focused on fading to Brynhildr's tent. She knew she had to get ready herself and take a deep breath for what she was about to ask.

CHAPTER 18

"Hmm," Brynhildr said while taking a bite out of an apple. She swallowed and smiled knowingly at Fenryn. "I was wondering when I might see you again."

"I need your help." Fenryn sat across from the Valkyrie leader. "The ball is tomorrow. I am not fool enough to believe Apopis won't go. I want you to swear that if he captures me, you will wait two weeks and then kill me."

Brynhildr paused mid-bite. She set the dripping apple down on the wooden table in front of her. "How would I do such a thing if you are captured?"

"Don't play coy with me. Everyone knows that Valkyries will be destroyed if captured. Imbue me with the same spell you place on your foot soldiers. My timeline for escape is two weeks. If I can't do it by then, there truly is no hope. I want you kill me."

"Does your mate know what you ask of me?" Brynhildr's voice was firm even as her eyes gleamed with unshed tears.

Fenryn took a dagger from her boot and cut deep

into her palm. She extended both the dagger and her palm to her former leader. "Swear upon it."

Brynhildr swallowed, took the dagger, and sliced it into her own palm. Fenryn firmly grasped the other woman's bleeding hand.

"I swear, Fenryn. If you are taken, you will have two weeks to escape." Brynhildr did not falter as she shook Fenryn's hand. Her brown eyes held Fenryn's as golden light swirled around them, sealing their oath.

"Thank you." Fenryn stood up. The cut on her hand began sealing quickly. "I hope the Valkyries find their way to the ball tomorrow. Consider this your formal invitation."

Brynhildr's smile failed to reach her eyes. "We will be there, armed to the brim."

Fenryn grinned and bared her teeth. "I would expect nothing less. You never know when things might get messy."

Brynhildr took a final bite of her apple as Fenryn faded back to Marron's room. Marron was gone, but a breakfast tray was left on the table near the fireplace.

I'm back, She sent down the bond.

Welcome, I'm in the training yard. Have breakfast if you haven't yet. I'll be back soon.

Fenryn took a bite out of the bagel from the tray in front of her. The taste of tart orange jam exploded in her mouth with every bite. It was a bright and welcome joy paired with the dark coffee she was drinking. She decided to work on her glamour skills and attempt to skew her scent. She stared at the mirror and focused on her hair first. She glamoured blonde curls which stopped at her shoulders, tan skin, and crystalline blue eyes. Next, she altered her height to be closer to Meraena's. Changing her scent was a challenge. Instead of trying to create multiple fragrances, she focused solely on a lilac scent. She concentrated, bringing to mind blooming lilac fields in the early summer season.

She withdrew a simple blue dress from her duffel and studied her reflection. Marron threw open the door drenched in sweat. He began talking about dinner plans when his eyes landed on the petite woman in front of him. Marron frowned and looked behind him, then gazed around the room in confusion. He placed a hand on the hilt of the dagger resting on his right hip. "No. I don't know what kind of joke you think you're playing or who put you up to this, but you need to leave my room right now. You're in the wrong room, and if by chance you think you're in the right one, then you're still in the wrong room. Get out."

Fenryn grinned and willed her voice into a lower, huskier register. "Are you sure about that? I was promised you would enjoy my company while your mate is gone."

Marron seethed with anger. "Tell me who told you this and I will see them dealt with. My mate would eat you for dinner. *Leave.*" His voice was a guttural growl.

Fenryn smirked as she shifted back into her original form. "I masked my scent." She grinned with complete triumph.

Marron roared and tackled her, sending them both tumbling to the ground. She laughed and fought to escape his embrace.

"No, you're mine now." His mouth crushed hers in a heated kiss. His erection pressed into her hips as he ground against her.

"I am my own," she declared, throwing the prince off. She stalked towards him again, threw her dress above her head and met his lips with a demanding kiss of her own.

Marron groaned into Fenryn's mouth as her tongue skated against his bottom lip and her hands dug into his hips.

"I intend to have you in my bed today, Fenryn." He took control of the kiss and angled them towards his grand mattress.

Her legs collided with the plush comforter. She hesitated and waited for Marron to – Hel, she didn't know what she waited for, but she did.

Marron lifted her effortlessly and set her on the edge of the bed. "If you want me to stop, Ryn, tell me. You're in control here."

She swallowed and gave him a tight nod. "Don't stop."

"Thank the gods," Marron groaned. He climbed on top of her, his blazing skin meeting her blazing skin. She could not remember how to breathe. Every inch of Marron's body pressed against her. She craved it all.

Their tongues collided as Marron's mouth found hers. Heat roared in her core. She could feel her flame begging to break free. Marron's hands roamed along her body until they found their mark just between her thighs.

"Marron," she moaned into his mouth.

"Fuck me." He ground against her. "You're so wet."

"Some would take that as a hint, *prince*." Fenryn lifted her hips so his fingers could press further into her.

"So impatient." He nipped at her ear and replaced his hand with exactly what Fenryn's body had been craving.

"Marron!" She grabbed his back as if it would save her from the unnerving pleasure and slight pain that surged through her.

"Gods, Ryn." Marron grabbed the headboard and fought the desire to lose all control and ravage the woman gracing his bed.

"I'm okay." Fenryn reached up and laid a hand on his cheek. "I'm okay. I want this. I want you. I want all of you, just as you are."

"Are you sure?" *Gods, talking was difficult,* Marron thought.

"Absolutely." Fenryn ran her fingers through his tousled hair. "You won't break me."

He leaned down and kissed the ever-loving fuck out of his mate as he filled her completely. Fenryn gasped and gripped the sheets tightly to spare Marron's back from her nails. There was no restraint left. Marron gave way to the lust and desire that had been building in his body.

Fenryn savored the ecstasy of sex with Marron. Every part of her body reacted to his. She could feel her skin tightening and her abdomen clenching as her breathing became more and more ragged. She felt like she would never get enough. She stroked Marron's muscular chest as he drove into her. Soon they both called each other's name as they both found oblivion simultaneously. Fenryn had never even thought that climaxing together like this was possible; up until now, she thought it was only a story made up for young girls to agree to marriage.

Catching his breath, Marron laid beside her and

placed a tender kiss on her forehead. "I apologize if I…
hurt you."

She hit his chest with the back of her hand. "You
did no such thing. That's the last time you'll ever have
a remorseful thought about us having sex.
Understood?" She stared him down, waiting for his
submission.

He chuckled and pulled her to his chest, "Yes,
princess."

"How do I make you quit calling me that?" She
grumbled.

"You don't." He smiled and kissed the back of
her head. Fenryn could feel the warmth of his breath
tickling her neck.

Suddenly she shot out of bed in alarm. "Shit!
What time is it? I forgot about my training with
Meraena!"

Marron laughed and pulled her back down.
"Relax. Evan shot me a text to let me know that she was
still asleep. She gets pretty exhausted after hunting,
especially when her bloodlust gets as bad as last night.
She will be there at two."

Fenryn dropped back down onto the bed. "Thank the gods." She rolled to her side and placed a hand on Marron's chest, playing with the dark hair that covered his muscles. They laid in peace for a long while, simply enjoying each other's embrace.

"When you are ready to share more about your past, Ryn, I will listen." Marron kissed her forehead.

The last week I spent with Apopis was wretched. I wish I could forget it with every fiber of my being, Marron. She couldn't bring herself to speak out loud.

The prince held Fenryn as she told him of her final days with Apopis.

A demon approached Fenryn in the dungeon. "Clean yourself. Apopis wants your company tonight." The demon released the iron manacles from Fenryn's raw ankles. They were worn and bloody, no longer covered with fur or muscle. The manacles had worn past to the bone.

She dragged her aching body to the bath house in the slave quarters. She had been moved to the shadow realm. Maybe it had another name, but everything was cold and dark here. She knew it existed between the

Waters of Nu and Egypt. Regardless, no one seemed to hear the screams of the slaves and prisoners. Or if they did, they had long since given up caring.

A tiny woman with matted red hair approached Fenryn's wolf form with a bucket and a rag. "I will care for you. Rest."

A pathetic whimper escaped Fenryn's maw as she dropped down to the biting cold of the stone floor.

"You burned the demon king this morning. Your flame... I don't think his iron is enough to sever its power." The woman's whispers were so quiet as to be almost imperceptible. "He is running out of ways to hold you."

Fenryn's eyes closed.

"We pray to all the gods we know. Ours, yours, even the gods of strangers. Perhaps someone will finally listen."

Hecate! Fenryn called with the last of her might. Hecate, her sworn blood-sister. Hecate, who brought her to the Valkyries after Tyr was killed.

The world was lost to Fenryn for some time. When she awoke, every slave in Apopis' realm – man, woman, and child – surrounded her. She knew Apopis had entered the keep.

"Well, isn't this nice? You have a following. Such insignificant admirers." Apopis flicked his wrist casually. Twenty slaves huddled in formation burst into a mist of blood, splattering the horrified fae behind them. The shattered screams of the victims' families and loved ones echoed through the walls.

Fenryn stood on trembling legs. A guttural roar boomed from her chest.

"Terrifying." Apopis sneered. His demons formed a line of mist and glowing red eyes behind him as he approached her.

With the last of her strength, Fenryn willed a shield of flame to circle her and the slaves surrounding her.

"You think fire will stop me? You're just as weak as the rest of them." Apopis moved to walk through the fire, but his movement was met with the combined strength of every powerful defense the slaves had: fire, rain, acid, and inanimate objects from the dungeon surged through the air, shields of will and air-

the only defenses and power the slaves could access anymore.

Fenryn's legs quaked as the last of her energy gave way. She glanced at what she swore was Hecate, clad in ivory and gold armor, descended from the sky in an electric blaze of her own flaming power. For a moment, everyone was frozen in time- held in Hecate's power.

"Fenryn." Tears ran down her friend's cheeks and leaked from under her helmet. "I would have come sooner if I'd known."

"Save them. These people, save them! Kill me." Fenryn requested while avoiding Hecate's eyes.

"I will protect you all." Hecate placed a gentle hand on Fenryn's battle-weary shoulder. "They will be safe, and you will be given time to heal."

"Two hundred years for me and my people to heal ourselves and rebuild our lives. I don't know that I feel healed, but Hecate saved us."

"By the way that woman tended to you, I think you protected a great many of them. You called in Hecate. You saved them."

Fenryn closed her eyes and laid her head on his chest. She breathed in his now-familiar scent of cedar and flames, committing it to memory.

"When did you meet Hecate?" Marron continued to play with Fenryn's hair as they lay naked in each other's arms.

"Gods, I don't remember. It was sometime during my training with Tyr. Hecate never cared for formalities, even before the peace treaties were signed. She wanted to explore the realms and consequences be damned. We spent so many nights sneaking out and fading to different realms. She enjoyed Asgard and the Valkyries very much. She's always favored women."

"Have you ever...?" Marron paused, stroking her hair.

She laughed. "No, I took my training too seriously. I wanted to be the next Brynhildr. I had no time for romance or marriage."

"Sex isn't always romance," Marron hedged.

"True, and I've certainly experienced my fair share of advances. Some even from Hecate, but I was never in a place to give in."

"So, you were a virgin when you were handed over to Apopis?"

She nodded and listened to his thundering heartbeat.

"I'll kill him. I'll rip his bones from their joints until he begs me for the mercy of death."

"No." Fenryn gripped his chin. "His death is mine."

Marron kissed her then, grabbing hold of her hips. He wanted to devour the brazen woman the fates had blessed him with as a mate. Their bodies found each other once more and joined together in ecstasy. Later, as they laid tangled in each other's limbs, Fenryn's phone pinged through the ragged sound of their breath.

"I'll meet you in the fields in 10 minutes."

Fenryn extricated herself from Marron's strong arms and smiled at the prince. "Are you coming to training?"

He ran a hand down the curve of her waist slowly down her thigh, mesmerized by the movement. "I'm with you, Ryn. Always."

She bent to kiss his forehead. He wrapped his

arms around her waist, pulling her back down on top of him. Kissing her slowly as his hands roamed her body, Marron mumbled, "We can be twenty minutes late."

Fenryn laughed as she kissed him back. "Have you ever kept Meraena waiting? I don't get the impression she would handle tardiness well."

Grumbling, Marron buried his head in the crook of her neck. "She does not."

Fenryn stroked his red curls. "Then, you have to let me go."

A foreboding rumble coursed through Marron's chest. "Never."

CHAPTER 19

They made it with thirty seconds to spare. The Phrygirian fields were vastly different in that there were no berserkers screaming and losing their minds in the background. Green grass covered the ground instead of the trampled dirty ground of Asgard's training ring. Fenryn inhaled the warm summer air around her and noted the smell of blooming jasmine on the wind.

Thank you for sharing your past with me. Marron brushed the back of her hand as they waited for Evan and Meraena to fade in. *I was once married as well.*

Fenryn's head snapped up as she stared at the prince.

Marron gazed at the trees lining the edge of the training field. *Emalyn. I was young, she was a berserker in our guild. I thought we were surely mates. After the war for Scynthia was over, I married her in Asgard. I didn't even think of approaching my father. I had forgotten I was a prince in a way. I'd allowed myself to believe I was truly just one of the berserkers. We lived happily in Asgard for several years until I received a summons to return to Phrygia. Midas annulled the marriage without my permission and Emalyn was brought to the throne room before I could fade away to Asgard.*

Marron swallowed hard. Fenryn held his hand tightly. Tears stung her eyes as she pieced together what was to come.

Midas said it was a lesson to teach me my place. He said he would be the one to find me my match. He wanted my marriage to further the country's diplomatic efforts. He turned Emalyn to gold, but I wouldn't leave her side. I was wasting away in the throne room. Eventually he had her melted down. It wasn't until I cleared our home in Asgard that I learned she was four months pregnant. She was going to tell me the night she was taken.

Cold chills ran down Fenryn's spine. *You, Meraena and Evan. It's more than a friendship.*

Marron's heartbroken eyes held hers. *It's the beginning of a court of hope. I've been plotting to overthrow Midas ever since that night. He has a protection spell always guarding him. Anyone who wishes him harm within ten feet immediately turns to ash. He is untouchable. I could leave the kingdom, but then who would protect the citizens? It's been ten years since he murdered Emalyn. I've been able to hold him at bay for now, but who knows how long his guilt will last?*

Fenryn kissed his cheek. *We will figure this out, I promise.*

Meraena danced over to Fenryn and Marron, a brilliant smile lighting her face. "One tiny demi-siren ready to wipe the field with your demi-giant ass."

Fenryn grinned and squeezed Marron's hand in parting before she left to follow Meraena.

Evan stood on the edge of the field with his arms folded and his brow furrowed. "I don't like bringing the enemy here, or the fact that we don't even know if he will show. This all just feels wrong, Marron. I can't tell you why, but I feel like there's something we're missing here."

"I don't know what else we can do to prepare short of finding a psychic or calling on the fates,"

Marron replied. He watched the two women as they sparred. Meraena seemed to have the upper hand on Fenryn, an advantage of her lithe body. "We are so disconnected from the Egyptian deities here because of their refusal to sign the peace treaties. I know very little of their capabilities. Besides, our own time to prepare has been practically non-existent."

Evan shook his head and studied Fenryn's movements as she countered each maneuver Meraena threw her way. "I don't think it will be Apopis alone. Yes, it's more than likely that he will arrive. But I'm telling you, Marron – someone else has a hand in this. I can *feel* it."

Marron placed a hand on Evan's shoulder. "I hear you. I will keep my eyes and ears open."

Fenryn threw up a hand and met Meraena's attack with an invisible shield wall. Meraena hissed and bared all her fangs. Marron and Evan motioned to move forward.

"How far can you extend that?" Evan called out as he gathered his long hair into a tight bun and prepared to enter the field.

"I don't know. I was just wondering if I can make a physical shield similar to my mental one," Fenryn replied. She threw her arm out towards Marron. "Try and reach him, Evan."

Evan shifted into his berserker form and charged forward, only to be thrown onto his ass on the ground. He snarled at Marron, who was entirely too busy grinning at Fenryn to notice.

You look like a gaping fish. If you do that tomorrow, you will get yourself killed. Fenryn glared at the man as he stalked towards her. Muscles tensed, jaw tightened, heart racing: desire was evident in every movement.

Then it's a good thing you surprised us all today. Despite their audience, Marron's lips crashed into hers. He pulled her into an embrace that left nothing to the imagination.

Fenryn returned the kiss and decided to test one more theory. As she threw her arms around Marron's neck and wrapped her legs around his waist, she willed a wall of obsidian to encircle them. Suddenly, everything around Fenryn and Marron became very dark.

"Aren't you clever?" Marron rumbled into her neck as his mouth trailed kisses down to her breasts.

"Marron, I was training –" Fenryn's breath caught as Marron backed her into the wall, she had just willed into being.

"You were doing a wonderful job, princess," he nipped at her ear. "Bring down your wall if you're ready to stop." Marron's hands slipped down her waist and cupped her ass.

I don't want to stop.

Then don't. Marron pressed her further against the wall and raised his hands into her silken black hair.

She moaned as he thrust against her heated core. "We should."

Marron chuckled and stepped away, allowing Fenryn to slide down. She tried to ignore the feelings in her body and willed the wall away with a shaky breath. It slowly faded into smoky mist in the air.

Meraena gave them an all-too-knowing grin as Evan examined the air around them.

"That was amazing." Evan approached Fenryn

and Marron, whose hair was now down and mussed. Something akin to glee painted his speech. "We couldn't hear anything you said on our side. Could you hear us slamming into the wall from out here? Could you feel it?"

Fenryn shook her head and blushed. "I wasn't exactly paying attention."

Meraena laughed and looped her arm through Fenryn's by the elbow. "I think that was enough training for today. We are going to get snacks and pick up Fenryn's dress."

Marron laughed and shook his head as he walked with Evan towards the keep. Soon they were deep in discussion, likely thinking up battle strategies for Fenryn's newfound powers.

CHAPTER 20

Fenryn shifted into a glamour of a red-haired girl as she walked away with Meraena.

"I would love a slice of chocolate cake, like the ooey-gooey kind." Fenryn wiggled her fingers and moaned at the thought.

"Oh, yes. I absolutely agree." Meraena didn't wait for permission before she faded them to a bakery just outside of Hades's realm.

Fenryn took in their new surroundings with a quirked eyebrow. She noted how at ease the walking passerby seemed to be, despite the Underworld being merely twenty feet away.

"Persephone brought peace and comfort to Hades's realm. There's so much *life* here now," Meraena explained as they entered a bright pink and floral bakery.

Everything in the bakery was clearly themed after Hades and Persephone's pairing. The tiles on the floor were checkered in their colors, gray-blue and hot pink. The tables in the bakery alternated between those colors as well.

"Hey Tim!" Meraena called to the cashier at the register as she skipped to the counter. She leaned on the edge and said, "We need two Death By Chocolates, with two glasses of pomegranate wine for us both."

Fenryn hesitated before letting the giggle bubbling inside of her slip past her lips. "Puns? Seriously? Are we going to be trapped in the Underworld too?"

"Hades has a morbid sense of humor, but I love it," Meraena smirked.

Tim set their order on the counter. The two women brought it over to a lovely pink table adorned with blue stools.

"Why haven't you completed the mate bond with Marron yet?" Meraena asked as soon as Fenryn filled her mouth with cake.

Fenryn coughed and covered her mouth with a napkin before taking a sip of wine. The carbonation bit her tongue. "I don't know." She cleared her throat. "I can't ask you three for anything more than what we've prepared for tomorrow. Marron doesn't deserve that, to bear the repercussions of my past." Fenryn looked down at her plate and pushed around several crumbs with her fork. "I also don't know what I should do to complete the bond. We don't really plan for mates in Asgard, never mind talk about it. I never listened to those lessons in school anyway."

Meraena's jaw dropped, wine glass halfway to her mouth. "Seriously? Wow. Okay. Well, your scents are mixed, so that's always a good sign. But you have to establish a blood bond where you claim one another, just as the fates willed. Sex traditionally comes after, but I doubt any of us mates waited."

Fenryn took a thoughtful bite of her cake and allowed the chocolate to melt in her mouth. She pondered Meraena's words carefully. "Thank you."

"Anything else you need pointers on?" Meraena wiggled her eyebrows, her mouth full of cake as well.

Fenryn choked on her wine. "No, I think I'm okay for the moment."

"Well, if you ever do, I'm here." Meraena grinned all too sweetly as she finished her cake.

They finished their post-training snack and

faded into Aurelia's now-familiar boutique. Unlike last time, the store was now incredibly empty. Almost every dress rack in the room was bare.

Aurelia huffed at the door chime. "I don't suppose either of you know why the entirety of the Valkyries' battalion just came in and asked to purchase anything and everything suitable for a formal ball?"

Fenryn blushed. "It must be a really special occasion for them to deign showing up."

Meraena shot a level look at Fenryn. She sensed there would be frank conversation with Aurelia later. "You must be relieved that your business is thriving throughout the realms," Fenryn added quickly.

Aurelia waved the flattery off, strands of fabric floating behind her arm in the movement. "Of course, it is. No one compares to my dresses' craftsmanship. I never had a doubt." She pointed a tiny finger aggressively at Fenryn. "Your dress is ready. Go to the dressing room and I will bring it over."

Fenryn decided not to risk asking any extra questions. She headed to the dressing room and was promptly met by Aurelia, who was practically drowning under a gigantic gown bag.

"You cannot try on my masterpiece dressed like that. Strip." The woman hung up the bag on the door and crossed her arms in wait.

Fenryn nodded and followed her orders dutifully. Aurelia unzipped the bag and perfection spilled out.

"Yes, yes, I know." Aurelia assisted Fenryn as she stepped into the beautiful gown. "Now, I don't know for sure, but I think you could fit a sword diagonally down the back here. Your muscles might be stiff all night, but your dress will allow for it. Also, I can shorten the skirt should you wish to add more agility to your movement."

Fenryn paused her awestruck perusal to stare at Aurelia. The dressmaker touched the tip of her nose and smiled back. "Now, shoo. There will be no wrinkles or blemishes added to this masterpiece. I will deliver it to you in the morning."

Fenryn didn't waste time asking any further questions, though she desperately wanted to admire the way the light danced on the elegant dress's different fabrics. Never had she been so excited to don a dress for an event. She felt as if Aurelia had reached directly into her soul and discovered exactly what she desired.

By the time Meraena and Fenryn returned to the palace, Evan and Marron were in the prince's private study. The women found them watching a livestream of news from Egypt. Plagues had recently returned to the land, and black mist now covered the Nile near Cairo. Fae authorities were hard at work trying to relocate the humans in the area.

Her stomach turned. The chocolate cake she ate no longer offered her the comfort she wished for. She wrapped her arms around her abdomen. She could feel her breath becoming unsteady.

"I wonder if the Egyptian embassy received correspondence from Hecate before the plagues began," Fenryn mused aloud.

Marron approached Fenryn and wrapped her up in his arms. "We will bring an end to this."

"People are dying *right now*. It's already too late for them." Fenryn's chest shook with each breath she took. Fear was snaking its frozen claws around her ribs.

"We know Apopsis' power is back. As is yours." Evan began, pulling Meraena into his lap. "He is making a show of his power to draw you out. We must make our move tomorrow. This is a game for him, so we play smart. We play to win, Fenryn. It's best we keep our home advantage. We have plenty of allies surrounding us who are prepared to fight. We know your wolf can overtake him, and I believe Marron mentioned that your flame does damage to him as well. With everyone else fighting his demon army, and you and Marron tackling Apopis, we will win."

Fenryn wanted to believe him more than anything. She wished she could throw away every horror she had witnessed, but her memories suggested fighting her ex-husband would be anything but simple. Instead, she nodded and dropped her head to rest on Marron's shoulder. They watched the news broadcast about locusts and black mist carry on.

Everyone departed around midnight. Fenryn revealed she had invited the Valkyries to the ball and described to Marron and Evan how they had bought out Aurelia's shop. Marron and Evan discussed how having the battle-ready women go incognito could be an advantage. Fenryn fought the guilt that writhed in her gut for withholding the oath she made Brynhildr swear. *Hopefully, it won't be needed,* she thought to herself.

Later that night, Marron threw off his shirt and pants as he closed the door to his room. Fenryn's heart raced as she watched his muscles flex with each movement.

"I don't think I can. Not tonight." Fenryn dropped her eyes to the ground.

Marron lifted her chin with a gentle finger. "Not everything is about sex, Ryn." He gave her a soft smile. "I sleep in my boxers, sweetheart."

She blushed profusely and nodded.

He chuckled, his sapphire eyes dancing with humor. "Get comfortable, princess. I can't imagine sleeping in fighting leathers and a bra is comfortable."

Fenryn smirked and grabbed an oversized t-shirt from her duffel bag. She swallowed before turning her back to Marron. "Want to unzip me?"

A deep rumble sounded from Marron's chest as he stepped forward. He pushed Fenryn's long hair over her shoulder and placed a tender kiss on her neck as he slid the zipper down her back.

She pulled her leathers off and unfastened her bra, throwing on a much-too-large red graphic t-shirt with a picture of the Addams Family.

Marron looked at her and laughed. "Have you even seen the Addams Family?"

Fenryn threw her hands on her hips and glared at the prince. "Of course, I have. Wednesday is my spirit animal. There was this old woman who took me in for some years when I was stuck in my shifter form. She used to play black and white shows on TV all day. The Addams Family and the Munster's were my favorite."

Marron kissed the tip of her nose and climbed into bed. "Come on, princess."

She crawled into his open and waiting arms in bed. "You haven't pushed me to seal our mated bond," she said thoughtfully.

Marron stroked her back. "No."

"Why?" She traced the ward tattooed on his chest.

"There's too much going on, Ryn. It wouldn't

be fair to pressure you into that. We have time." He kissed the top of her head. "Whenever you are ready, I'll be here, but until then, I can wait."

Fenryn hugged his broad chest and held on as she fell asleep to the lullaby of his beating heart.

CHAPTER 21

The morning of the ball passed in a blur. Meraena arrived early and graced everyone with doughnuts and coffee. She kicked Marron out of his bedroom soon after and began work on Fenryn's "disastrously long hair." True to her word, Aurelia brought over the gown "with a few minor adjustments" sometime mid-morning. Marron and Evan secured the fortress along with King Midas. When lunchtime came around, Queen Damodice knocked on the door.

"Fenryn? May I speak with you?" The Queen beckoned.

Fenryn glanced at Meraena as she finished applying eyeliner to her lids. "Is that allowed?"

"I'm not the one with a mental link to the prince." Meraena tapped Fenryn's forehead with the makeup brush.

"Oh. Right." Fenryn blushed and reached out to Marron. *Do we trust your mother? She wants to speak to me.*

Marron was quick to reply. *Leave your shields*

down, but yes, let her speak with you.

Fenryn nodded and took a steadying breath. She opened the door for the queen and offered her a low curtsy. Meraena set down her makeup and followed suit.

"You two look lovely." The queen's voice was too stiff for the compliment to ring true. She wrung her hands nervously. "I don't know what you know about the politics of this kingdom, Fenryn, but my position as a queen is more of an object than a partner. I must rely on gossip and loose lips."

Fenryn nodded and tightened the belt of her robe. She relaxed once she felt the reassuring bite of her dagger held against her waist.

"I do not know my husband's plans, but I know he does not seek your well-being. The king has all but locked himself in his study the past few days. I can't help but think it must be intentional. Tread lightly today and trust no one. Marron's side of the keep is warded against evil, but the same cannot be said for the castle's gold-plated walls."

"I hear you." Fenryn gave a militant nod to

Queen Damodice, unsure what more she should say.

"Thank you." Meraena added.

That, Fenryn thought. *That was what I needed to say.*

Meraena is always the one to add a soft touch of manners when we forget typical courtesies are expected of us, Marron reassured her.

"Just focus on your survival," Queen Damodice said. "We shall consider it thanks enough." She assessed Fenryn and Meraena once more before she turned to leave.

"Well, fuck." Meraena threw her lipstick at the mirror. "I knew Midas was a prick, but dammit, couldn't he wait for his turn to strike us?"

Fenryn replayed the queen's message in her mind. She noted the timid body language she displayed. *Marron, someone needs to guard your mother. She wouldn't fidget as much if she was warded. Can we protect her somehow?*

Marron's response was chilling. *My mother was never allowed to bear wards on her person. If we appoint an independent guard to watch over her, it would raise a red flag for Midas.*

In that case I will attempt to shield her when I am in her presence, Fenryn decided. She sat back in front of the mirror to finish applying her blood-red lipstick.

Once that was done, Meraena and Fenryn helped each other slip into their ballgowns. Meraena's dress was a shimmering homage to her mer father. A corseted bodice of beautifully shimmering teal crystals fitted her curves and flowed delightfully out into a lavender tulle skirt with a scandalous high cut that climbed all the way up to the middle of her right thigh. A pair of shining ivory heels peeked out from under the tulle skirt.

"You look stunning," Fenryn smiled as she placed an amethyst crown atop Meraena's curls.

She smiled and shook her head. "You are the showstopper today, Fenryn."

Fenryn blushed as she looked at her reflection. Her dress was a mixture of deep emerald green and midnight black fabric. The colors melded together in a balance of filigree and gold metallic boning hugging her curves in a corset. Thin emerald-green sleeves covered her shoulder, leading into a plunging neckline that ended just above her sternum. The dress's fabric trailed behind her in a loose flowing train that couldn't decide if it was shimmering green or dark as night.

She slid her sword into the built-in sheath Aurelia had constructed inside her dress. She could feel the tip of her blade just below her hip. "I won't be able to sit down in this dress."

"We'll be too busy dancing anyway." Meraena opened the door. "Now, let's go find our men."

CHAPTER 22

Diplomats and politicians from numerous realms filled the courtyard of King Midas's palace that evening. Despite their gorgeous dresses, the Valkyries stood out among the crowd. The imposing figure they cut made it clear they were ready for any challenge. Brynhildr flexed her biceps in a toga-inspired dress that made a Greek diplomat break out in a sweat. There was no sign of Loki or the berserkers anywhere. They must have remained on the outskirts of the palace.

Music began to fill the air as Fenryn and Meraena joined their waiting partners. Evan wore a purple suit so dark it almost passed as black. His tie was a shade of lilac that matched Meraena's hair and his own smoldering eyes.

Marron paused mid-conversation as his gaze fell on Fenryn. He swallowed hard and simply walked away from the conversation he was having.

You look like a delicious threat, princess. He took her hand in his and kissed her knuckles.

Fenryn blushed. "Thank you. I hope your

company isn't easily offended."

"They'll understand." Marron wrapped an arm around her waist. He paused as his hand brushed against the steel strapped to her back.

Fenryn grinned. "Aurelia thought it might be handy to have a weapon readily available."

Marron kissed her temple. "She thought you may need wards to protect you as well," he whispered in her ear. "There are wards and spells woven into the gold boning wrapped around your breasts."

"Are you staring, prince?" Fenryn stepped back and placed a hand on her chest in mock outrage.

"Absolutely," Marron growled and kissed her full on the mouth. "I am yours, Ryn, as the fates see fit."

Her heart skipped a beat as he began the first step of the claiming oath.

Fenryn opened her mouth to reply as King Midas slowly stood up from his golden throne, bracing himself on both arms. A courtier silenced the crowd and called attention to the King's words.

"As you all know, my son Marron has been blessed with a mate by the fates. Fenryn, daughter of

Loki, has been given the honor of this role. As a gift to bless their union, I arranged for Hel to allow a short visit of Fenryn's departed godfather, Tyr!"

Indeed, the man who now walked down the aisle was the Norse god of war and justice. Tyr's long brown hair hung almost to his shoulders and brushed the old Asgardian leathers he used to wear for training with Fenryn. The god held out his right hand to Fenryn. "Dance with me."

Fenryn could feel Marron trying to speak through their mental bond, but her shields were up and held firm. Tears pricked the back of her eyes. She fought the lump in her throat as she placed her hand in Tyr's.

A slow waltz began playing from the stage orchestra. Tyr held Fenryn with his right arm as he led the dance.

"My, how you've grown, child." Tyr chuckled and tucked a curl behind Fenryn's ear as they danced.

"I would hope so. Two hundred fifty years is a long time. You spoke to me in the river, when I ran through the fields with Marron. How?" She searched his brown eyes.

"I begged Hel for a chance to see you again. I just needed to know you were okay." Tyr hugged Fenryn close to his chest with both arms.

Fenryn's heart faltered. She threw an invisible shield over her friends and the ball's other attendees. She withdrew her sword from her dress and pressed it to Tyr's throat with no hesitation.

"I bit off Tyr's *left* arm as a pup. If you're going to impersonate my mentor, you better know damn well what he looks like," she growled and shoved her blade fiercely into the imposter's neck. Yet the midnight skin resisted the impact of her blade.

Apopis' façade melted away as he stood grinning behind Fenryn's blade. "You're right. But truly I didn't care enough to bother. It was Midas' idea, to impersonate the bastard god. I just wanted you, darling."

Black talons wrapped around her sword. Fenryn willed her fire to consume the blade, but instead an unnervingly dark liquid seeped out from the grasp.

"Come home and play with me. There's so

much we have left to accomplish." Apopis ran his other black as night hand down her cheek, sending chills down her back.

Fenryn could see Marron shouting as he threw himself against her shield.

"Pity you won't let your little gang play with us. It would be such fun." Apopis snapped his fingers and brought several diplomats on the other side of the shield to their knees.

Fenryn screamed with rage as she pushed her blade into Apopis' neck.

He dissipated into his trademark black mist and tsked. "That's no way to treat your husband, *dear*."

Fenryn shifted to her wolf form. The Valkyries all discarded their dresses to reveal battle leathers, wings, and weapons beneath.

"Damn it, Apopis. We all dressed up for tonight," Brynhildr chided. "Remove the shield, Fenryn. It means little to him."

Fenryn snarled and dropped the protective barrier. Marron shifted and ran to her side. They both charged Apopis as the Valkyries and Meraena worked to protect the innocent bystanders. Meanwhile, Evan rushed King Midas and Queen Damodice. Remembering her vow, Fenryn maintained a shield around the queen as long as she possibly could.

Apopis laughed as he faded away from Fenryn. "This is child's play, and yet… Did none of you think of how Asgard is now left unattended?"

Fenryn skidded to a stop.

What the fuck are you doing? We can kill him! Move, Ryn! Marron shouted in her mind. His wolf form snapped at her as he ran past and tackled the Demon King to the ground. Apopis simply wrapped his arms around Marron's core. He tightened his stronghold, trapping the wolf in his grasp, until an unearthly snapping sound rang out.

Marron? Marron! Fenryn's cry was met with unnerving silence.

"No!" Queen Damodice screamed and fell to her knees.

Meraena left the Valkyries and rushed to Marron's side.

Fenryn raged forward and bit the bastard demon king's

despicable face. He kicked her in the stomach, throwing her to the side as he climbed back to his feet. Black blood poured down his face. Where was Loki? Where were Phrygia's soldiers? Fenryn tore into him with her claws as she screamed into the void where Marron's mind once was.

Get up! I am yours. I am yours, just as the fates willed it, Marron! Marron!

"That's enough," Apopis roared as he grabbed Fenryn by the throat. "We are going home!"

Apopis immediately faded them back to the hellhole of the Nu's waters. Fenryn fought his grip clawing at his obsidian skinned arm. Her fur caught fire, as she begged her body to fade anywhere else – anywhere but this realm. Apopis talon clawed hand collided ferociously with her maw as the flames seared his palm.

Fenryn realized that something was holding her in Apopis' grasp. She caught a glimpse of a new talisman in his clutches. A pendant of pure gold with an amethyst set in its center was wrapped around his wrist. Though she cursed the demon king, her mind immediately began plotting. She knew she had exactly two weeks to escape before her pact with Brynhildr took effect.

Acknowledgements

This book would not be possible without my amazing support system. That begins with my patient and loving husband, Zachary, who has encouraged me every step of the way. Next, I have to give a huge shout out to my mom, Amy, who did a final walk through with edits and helped me figure out the inner workings of Microsoft Word. Thank you to all my amazing readers and supporters. Shannon F., this wouldn't have been nearly as coherent without your feedback. I love you all. I hope you enjoyed A Cruel Game of Fate and keep watching for the upcoming sequel!

MARRON'S BONUS SCENE

Marron sat on a well-used, albeit, sticky, swivel bar stool as he chugged his third mug of beer, drowning out the day's past torments. Kornelia had declared that she could not be wed on dry land, and to do such would break the esteemed traditions of water nymphs everywhere.

Garrett, the Thursday night bartender, cleared his throat. "If you do not wish the world to know that Prince Marron is frequenting Margot's, you may want to fix your glamour."

Marron grumbled as he tossed back the end of his drink and adjusted his glamour, hiding his identity. "You have no clue, man. I have never had a day like this. My father arranged my marriage- out of nowhere." He swung his arms wide, knocking over a centaur's glass of wine, earning an irritated glare. "And *then*, my friend brings home this stray…*thing.*"

Marron handed Garrett his mug, hoping for a refill.

"Do you have someone I can call?" Garrett hedged, slowly pouring the lightest ale into the cup.

"No. I," He said, emphatically placing a hand on his chest. "Am fine!"

With his fresh ale, Marron stood from his seat and went to join the crowd on the dance floor. It didn't take long for a succubus to find him. She wrapped her slender arms around his broad shoulders.

"Care to dance?" She practically sang.

"I can't." Marron tapped the tip of her nose. "I think I am mated to a cat."

The succubus stared at Marron in pure confusion before shaking her head and moving along.

"Alright, Marron. I think you've had enough." Evan pulled Marron's limp arm over his shoulder.

"Evan! I think the fates are playing a sick joke. I swear I feel connected to the creature in Meraena's apartment. I think it's my mate."

Evan shook his head and ushered the prince outside. "You're drunk. Everything will be clearer in the morning."

Marron leaned into his blood brother. "I never

wanted to marry again. I loved Emalyn."

Evan faded the prince to his barracks and laid him down on the nearest cot. "I know. We will weather the storms together, as we always have. Rest now."

MERAENA AND EVAN

BONUS SCENE

Her legs wrapped around his waist as she buried her face in the crook of his neck. "Take me to your apartment, Evan."

They faded from Meraena's front door instantly and Evan tossed his mate onto his huge bed.

Meraena squealed as she fell, laughing once she landed on the down comforter. "Lose the clothes, hotshot."

Evan's eyes gleamed at the order. "What do I get if I comply?"

Meraena's eyes shifted to those of a blood thirsty siren; her fangs descended. "I won't drink you dry."

Evan chuckled as he removed his jeans, throwing them towards the wall. "I'd like to see you try, sweetheart."

Meraena eyed the scars that lined his collar bone, denoting nearly every time they reunited after long periods of time apart. Her traitorous tongue snuck out and licked her lips in anticipation.

Without a second though, Evan grabbed either side of Meraena's designer dress and ripped it from her body.

A feral grin spread across Meraena's lips as their monsters found comfort in one another's chaos.

"I've missed you," she declared as Evan lowered himself to kneel between her thighs.

Placing a rough and biting kiss at the apex of her leg, Evan moaned as he gripped her flesh hard enough to elicit a gasp. "There are no words to the describe the void in my chest when we are apart. We should remedy that soon."

Meraena moaned as Evan's tongue found its mark. "Agreed."

Evan worked her body to the cliff of ecstasy and reached into the drawer of the bedside table, withdrawing a pair of leather handcuffs. "Arms up, sweetheart."

Meraena bit her lip, squeezing her legs together as she followed his instructions.

"That's my good girl." Evan bit her neck and positioned himself between her legs.

He wasted no time, filling her to the brim with his length.

A scream fell from her lips as she adjusted to him, but she wasn't given much time before he took her legs and placed them on his shoulders.

"Give me your hands, Mer." Evan moved with a rhythm that had Meraena tensing as she saw stars.

He gripped the center of the cuffs and held her arms captive against the headboard as he moved with her body. Gods she had missed him, missed their relationship, missed this.

With a final thrust, Meraena's body shook as the orgasm overtook her. Evan roared with his completion and collapsed on the bed breathless.

Eventually, Evan uncuffed her wrists and pulled Meraena into him, covering their bodies with his comforter.

"I have a new roommate," Meraena murmured already half asleep.

"Mm. Think there will be trouble?" Evan

wound a strand of Meraena's lilac curls around his finger.

"There usually is, but I think this one will be worth it." Meraena yawned as she snuggled into Evan's warmth.

"Then we will handle it as it comes. Sleep, love."

She was snoring before he finished his sentence.

FATE'S WICKED TRIALS

Marron reached out to Fenryn, caressing her fur. "Come on, Ryn. Shift for me."

She opened her swollen, crusted eyes to see Marron standing tall and unscathed. He wore a loose white button-up shirt, the top two buttons undone. Black slacks adorned his hips.

She frowned at the prince. Had she made it all up? Were they safe? Glancing around, they were in an unfamiliar bedroom, and everything was dark. Black linens lined the windows, and the fireplace burned low as she lay trembling on a threadbare rug.

"We are at a local tavern. Phrygia is not safe for us. We had to run." Marron sat next to her, crossing his legs. "Can you shift for me, love?"

She bared her teeth. Marron *never* called her love.

The facade faltered. The illusion of heat disappeared and was replaced with the icy sting of the stone floors she had grown to hate so many years ago.

Her wolf snarled, baring its sharp teeth with a

vicious snap.

"I tried." Apopis sighed apathetically, brushing the dirt from his black slacks, the amulet still secured around his wrist. "As soon as you are done being stubborn, I have a room prepared for you. We will do things differently this time. I *need* you, Fenryn. My demons need a queen to lead them. A king is only half of the equation."

A low growl vibrated from her chest as she rose in her chains.

"Starvation and dehydration will change your mind." Apopis shrugged and buttoned his gaping shirt with his talons, leaving the dungeon.

Despite the chains, Fenryn lunged for the god, roaring with hate.

Marron. Please. She swore she could feel the bond, weak—yes—but still present.

There was nothing in return. No quick wit, no name-calling, just an echoing abyss. Fenryn howled her heartache to the dungeon walls. They listened.

Marron

The Valkyrie healer came to him first. He

wasn't sure who she was, but she made mention of something being broken and something vital having been punctured.

He blacked out after that.

When he woke, he was in Meraena's apartment, surrounded by Evan, Meraena, and his mother?

He frowned at the queen and then the others. Hopefully, someone understood his confusion.

Meraena answered. "Your heart. Gods, it was so close, Marron. Calliope saved you. Once we got you to your room and healed enough, we faded you here. No one except us can enter right now. Your mother demanded entry. She still has Fenryn's shield around her. No one knows how."

"Where?" Marron croaked. Gods, it hurt to breathe, to talk, to move.

Evan observed his wince. "Your ribs were severely cracked. You're regrowing your rib cage."

"Where is my mate?" He demanded.

Everyone avoided his gaze.

"Dammit." Marron went to stand. "Where is she!"

"Enough." His mother placed a gentle hand on his shoulder, the shield but a thin barrier between her touch. "Apopis took her. Just before the ball, your father gave him an enchanted talisman to protect him from physical harm, such as her claws and fire. I saw it on his dresser as we got ready and then on Apopis during the fight. I tried to warn Fenryn."

Ryn. I'm alive. I will come for you.

It was as if he was speaking to himself. Marron wanted to scream. How could he have failed her? How did she end up in Apopis' realm again?

"Loki? The berserkers?" Marron looked at Evan.

The general dropped his head, long brown hair covering his face. Meraena placed a gentle hand on his back. "They were surrounded by that black fog we saw on the news in Cairo. It held thousands of shadow demons. We lost so many… Loki returned to Asgard to protect as many of its citizens as possible, but Apopis was just using that as a distraction for them. He knew it would work."

Marron huffed and nodded. "What of Midas?"

"He has locked himself in the castle. Not even your mother can return. He anticipates war from all of us." Evan glared at no one in particular, rage visibly pulsing through his veins.

"His time has come." Marron seethed, groaning from pain as he let his head fall back onto the pillow. Memories of Emalyn, his late wife, flashed through his mind. Her guttural scream as Midas turned her and his unborn child to golden nothing still tormented his mind when he thought of the malicious king.

"I will be the one to do it." His mother's soft voice broke through the silence.

Meraena nodded. "Good. You deserve his kill." Her eyes turned blood red on the last word.

Evan sighed. "Go to Asgard, Mer. The Valkyries likely have someone for you."

Meraena glared at him, likely trying to determine whether arguing would get her anywhere, but she faded without hesitation.

"Hecate heard from the Egyptian embassy." Evan began staring at Marron's chest.

"And?" he rasped. Marron was running out of

energy to stay awake.

"Ra is the god in charge. He also has had dealings in the past with Apopis. He wants to meet with you before going to the Waters of Nu."

"Bring…Him…Now." Marron lost the fight to the exhaustion of his healing body.

Fenryn

There was no light in the crypt where she was being held. Every now and then, a shadow demon would enter. She assumed their purpose to determine if she had changed forms yet. That was the marker of time she used, though. She lasted 36 visits before hunger and dehydration consumed her.

Fenryn's wolf gave in, and she shifted to her fae form. She lay on the damp stones, shivering in the ball gown Aurelia designed specifically for her. No weapons were left, yet its gold boning stayed. The dress hung loosely on her body now, her curves having given way to hunger.

"Master will see you washed and fed." A fae male remarked as he unlocked the chains.

She took in his scent and stature. Overall, he

smelled of earth and possibly decay, but it was so subtle it could easily be mistaken for petrichor. "Who are you?"

"A mistake." He kept his eyes down as he led her out of the dungeon. His hair and skin were all a dark shade of brown, not blackened or onyx as Apopis' spawn had all been rendered.

"Is that your name?" Fenryn held her dress tightly, keeping it from falling to her feet as they climbed a grand flight of stairs.

"I have no name. I am not supposed to be, and yet I am. Forget me. Your room is at the top of these stairs to the left, Lady Fenryn." He bowed lowly to her and vanished into the darkness of the stairwell.

Indeed, a room was prepared for a female of status at the top of the stairs. Fenryn refused to admit how out of breath she was by the time she made it there or how she had to crawl on her hands and knees to make it through the threshold. The room was decorated in dark gothic florals and filigree. A fireplace sat unlit in front of a plush black queen bed. A lace curtain cascaded down from the ceiling, covering the mattress on all sides. Hanging on the mantle was a dark pink, almost maroon, ball gown designed for Victorian-era events. Fenryn swallowed. If it was a game Apopis wanted to play, then she would give him one to end them all.

Digging deep in the drawers of the dresser, Fenryn found a black lace nightgown that landed mid-thigh. It would do.

Tearing the gold boning from her dress, she braided it into a makeshift choker necklace and donned the black heels Apopis had left to go with the dress. Glancing at her reflection in the mirror, Fenryn pursed her lips and threw her hair into an elegant, braided crown. She could make a statement, too.

A female demi-demon with blonde hair and violet eyes knocked on the door and balked as she took in Fenryn's state. Her ivory skin had an ombre effect as it shifted from porcelain to onyx at her elbows and knees. "Master left specific instructions…"

"He is not *my* master. You may take me to dinner." Fenryn ordered as she walked past the shocked female and waited in the hallway, arms crossed over her barely covered chest.

They walked in silence down the black-and-gold-lined hallway. Gilded sconces lit with blue flames lined the walls as they tread the familiar path to the dining room.

The iron doors were new, likely a boast of warning to Fenryn. She lifted her chin as they creaked open. Apopis was sipping on blood-red wine when his eyes caught her attire, and he spat viscously on the ground.

Fenryn strode to her seat at the far end of the table, keeping her head high and eyes on the meal lining the grand oak table. A blue flame lit the fireplace behind Apopis.

"I see you did not find your room." Apopis straightened his tie. "A pity. My servants must be forgetting their place." A dark glare shot to the woman who had escorted her into the room.

Fenryn cut into a rare slab of veal on her plate, her tone unscathed. "On the contrary, my room was lovely. Thank you."

Apopis glared at Fenryn as she ate the bloody

meat, his black knuckles turning uncharacteristically white as his fists tightened.

"I left you a perfectly decent dress." He threw back the contents of his wine, swallowing hard.

"Mmm," she ate the mashed potatoes slowly, hating herself for savoring the garlic and rosemary. "Perhaps, if I was Anne Boleyn."

Apopis faded to her side, clutching her neck, cutting off her air supply. "Do *not* test me."
Fenryn narrowed her eyes, waiting.

He released his hold, smoothed his suit, and returned to his seat. "We are to be remarried in a week. You will eat and be healthy by that time. To Hel with heirs, but you *will* bind yourself to me. You have fought me at every turn in that regard. Perhaps in time you will change your mind. However, we *will* rule this empire together."

Fenryn dropped her fork loudly. "I'd rather *rot.*" She spat in his face. "Put me back in those chains if this is your plan. Why in all the realms would you want me to rule this damned place with you?"

Apopis stared at her arm. A searing pain coursed

through the appendage. She gasped, clutching her wrist, seeing the now glowing infinity mark. "What happens when a mated bond is denied?"

She glared, holding her throbbing wrist.

"You will both go mad and die. I need a partner of either death or chaos. I want no death gods, and you were promised to me first. My demons favor and respect you for some gods-forsaken reason. The majority of the children are demigods or demons due to the insufferable slaves and your damned boned-etched ward. In your absence I had to make do with the ilk that was available. Alas, my children all become damned shadow demons after twenty years. There has been no hope for heirs. Rule with me, and we can bring the realms to their knees."

Fenryn laughed, priding herself and Hecate for their ingenuity in carving the spell on her pelvic bone. It was the best protection she had from him. "I don't want the realm on its knees."

"Then your mate will be driven insane, and the block in the bond—" He gestured to the mark burned into her wrist. "Neither of you will be able to feel or hear one another. You will curse him to his own misery and, ultimately, death."

Fenryn threw her knife at the god. It landed in his right shoulder but fell right out, the god's skin fusing back together instantaneously. The godsdamned talisman continued to protect him from her attacks.

"He's already dead." Tears stung the back of her eyes.

"Hm. I don't recall his last breath being recorded." Apopis idly ate a roasted potato.

Fenryn hid the emotion his statement stirred. "I will never join you."

"Give it time, Fenryn." Apopis waved his arms with unnecessary flare, and she was returned to her room without her meal. She threw herself at the door, screaming and cursing the demon king. The lock held, refusing to give. Not only was the door impossible to open, but the windows were barred with iron. It was just an upgraded dungeon.

She moved her attention to the brand. She willed her flames to ignite, yet nothing came. She begged her wolf to come out and was met with grating silence. She roared in frustration.

Turning to the fireplace, she added more logs to the dying embers. She waited for the flames to rise. Once they did, she took a deep breath and threw her marked arm into the heart of the fire. The flames danced around her wrist, avoiding her skin. In a fit of rage, she grabbed the hideous dress from the armoire and threw it into the fire. The flames burned bright as they devoured the fabric.

"I can help," a small voice announced from the corner near the ceiling.

Fenryn grabbed the first thing her hand made contact with, the fire poker, and aimed it in the direction of the voice. A small male pixie descended. He had to be a demi-demon, as his light was gray. Everything about him was gray.

"Who are you?" she asked.

"Name's Glitch." The male put a hand to his chest, then extended the minuscule extremity toward Fenryn. "Don't trust any of us demis. We are our own people until Apopis decides he has use for us. Presently, I am not needed."

Glitch put his tiny hand to his mouth and whispered, "He can basically override our bodies through possession. It's these damned brands." He floated closer, showing her the infinity mark on his small wrist.

Fenryn frowned at the pixie and allowed him to shake her finger. "Why are you gray?"

"Ah. I was born in the shadow realm, pocket realm, whatever you want to call it. The place that isn't. We are born fae, but after a while, we start to dull. Soon, I will be nothing more than a shadow demon." Glitch adjusted his shirt sleeves as he explained.

"Glitch is an unusual name." Fenryn grabbed the satin robe from the back of her door and wrapped the cool fabric around her.

"That's because I randomly fade to gods know where. Sometimes, I am with Morrigan. Sometimes, I visit Odin. Other times, I end up with the Aztecs. I have no control of my fading." Indeed, his body turned static, similar to what Fenryn had seen on television years ago, and then he was gone. It took ten minutes for Glitch to return, panting and paler than before.

"I'm sorry." Fenryn sat on the bed, staring at the brand on her wrist. "I thought I got everyone out with Hecate before."

Glitch took a stuttering breath, smoothing his curls behind his ears. "You got the slaves out. We abominations were hidden. No one knew of us, and we are many. Apopis was experimenting in trying to create an army, if you will."

"I'm so sorry." Fenryn met his eyes. "I would have fought for you all, too."

"You got our parents and siblings out. We know." Glitch straightened his back, grinned, and tightened his monochromatic bowtie. "Now, let's see to this brand. We can cut it off. It will heal in about three minutes, but if your mate bond is still there, you can at least send a signal that you are alive."

Fenryn shuddered at the thought. If there was a chance Marron was alive, she could do this. She *would* endure this. "Alright."

"Give me time to get a knife. I will return." He turned to static again and left Fenryn alone in her plush prison.

Throwing herself back onto the bed, she prayed to her father, wishing he'd rain destruction upon Apopis or send her some gift that would aid her in doing so. Closing her eyes, a silent tear escaped down her cheek, landing in her hair on the much too soft pillow.

"My Lady." Glitch cleared his throat. "I can only hold this dagger for so long before it eats away my hands entirely."

She surged forward and retrieved the blade, hissing as its iron blade seared her skin. The metal eating through her skin due to its poisonous qualities towards fae. "Thank you."

"His curses always return quickly. We've all tried to pry them away…" He bowed his head and faded as quickly as his static allowed.

She took a steadying breath and wrapped the hilt in the excess of the skirt, the bright red fabric a haunting premonition of the blood that would pour from her wrist. Clenching her teeth, Fenryn laid the blade against her skin, allowing it to burn before she began cutting the mark away.

She tried and failed not to scream; the curse mark went deep. Blood seeped out and around her arm, dripping onto the light pink bedding. Good. Let him know she would fight him. Close to fainting, Fenryn sent out her message.

Marron. I'm safe enough. Apopis needs me as his counterpart to rule. Please be alive. I am yours as the Fates willed it to be.

Fenryn! was the only thing she heard before she lost hold of consciousness and collapsed on the bed.

<u>**ABOUT THE AUTHOR:**</u>

JESSICA LANE LIVES IN CENTRAL MISSOURI WITH HER TWO BOYS, HUSBAND AND STEPDAUGHTER. SHE WORKS FULL-TIME AND WRITES IN HER FREE TIME. SHE ENJOYS HIKING AND DRINKING DELICIOUS COFFEE WITH FRIENDS. YOU CAN FOLLOW HER ON INSTAGRAM, FACEBOOK AND TIKTOK @JLYNNE-LANE OR JESSICA LANE-AUTHOR.

www.ingramcontent.com/pod-product-compliance
Lightning Source LLC
Chambersburg PA
CBHW070820170726
48000CB00019B/1479